by Henry Winkler and Lin Oliver

HANK ZIPZER

the world's greatest underachiever

The Night I Flunked My Field Trip

by Henry Winkler and Lin Oliver

HANK ZIPZER

the world's greatest underachiever

The Night I Flunked My Field Trip

Grosset & Dunlap
An Imprint of Penguin Group (USA)

Cover illustration by Tim Heitz

GROSSET & DUNLAP
Published by the Penguin Group
Penguin Group (USA), 375 Hudson Street, New York, New York 10014, USA

USA | Canada | UK | Ireland | Australia | New Zealand | India | South Africa | China
Penguin Books Ltd, Registered Offices: 80 Strand, London WC2R 0RL, England

For more information about the Penguin Group visit penguin.com

Text copyright © 2004 by Henry Winkler and Lin Oliver Productions, Inc.
Cover illustration copyright © 2013 by Penguin Group (USA). Interior illustrations
copyright © 2004 by Penguin Group (USA). All rights reserved. Published by
Grosset & Dunlap, a division of Penguin Young Readers Group, 345 Hudson Street,
New York, New York, 10014. GROSSET & DUNLAP is a trademark of
Penguin Group (USA). Printed in the U.S.A.

Library of Congress Control Number: 2004001430

ISBN: 978-0-448-43352-3   10 9 8 7 6 5 4 3 2 1

ALWAYS LEARNING   PEARSON

For Esther Newberg. Thank you for
making this your first children's book.
And Stacey, always—HW

For Leslie King and Teresa Nathanson,
precious friends and Pilgrim
mothers forever—LO

CHAPTER 1

"**Zip, don't tell me you forgot** your permission slip," my best friend Frankie Townsend whispered as we slid into our seats in Ms. Adolf's fourth-grade classroom.

"I didn't say I *forgot* it," I whispered back. "I said I *might* have forgotten it."

"Dude, I am not liking the sound of this," Frankie said, shaking his head.

I pulled my backpack onto the top of my desk and began a complete search for the permission slip.

"It's got to be here," I told Frankie as I unzipped my backpack and began looking through the main compartment.

"Zip, this is the last day—"

"I know," I interrupted, "to bring it in. The field trip is tonight. Why would I forget my permission slip?"

"Because you're Hank Zipzer, King of the Morons," answered a voice from the row behind me. It was Nick McKelty, the true king of the morons, who never misses a chance to hurl an insult my way. He laughed really loud and blasted some of his nasty dragon breath my way.

I know I forget a lot. I mean a lot, a lot. But I really wanted to go on this trip. And I didn't need McKelty on my case about it.

"Listen up, McKelty," I began. "I'm tired of you . . ."

The bell rang before I could continue. Ms. Adolf walked over to her desk and put her sack lunch into her bottom drawer. I sit close enough to her desk to smell that she was having something involving tuna fish. And a day-old banana. I can sniff out a day-old soft, turning-black banana a block away.

"That will be quite enough, Henry," Ms. Adolf said to me, tapping on her desk with this pointer stick she has.

Enough? I hadn't even started. If she only knew.

"But, Ms. Adolf, I didn't start this."

"Henry, if you keep talking, I'm going to send you to Principal Love's office."

Why was *I* getting into trouble? *McKelty* called *me* a moron. And why was she still calling me Henry when I've been telling her since September my name is Hank? Come on, this was April already. That's eight months of Henry and zero months of Hank. Even my orthodontist Dr. Gibbons started calling me Hank four months after I had asked him to, and he's deaf in one ear.

Ms. Adolf took the silver key she wears on a lanyard around her neck and unlocked the top drawer of her desk. She took out her roll book and carried it over to my desk. Opening the book, she ran her finger down the list of names, stopping at the very last one. I had a bad feeling about that, since my name is Zipzer, and it starts with the last letter of the alphabet.

Sure enough, Ms. Adolf looked at me over the top of her glasses and frowned. And I don't mean just a regular frown, either. She looked at me like there were worms crawling all over my face. Brown, hairy worms.

"Congratulations, Henry," she said in a voice that matched her face. "You are the only pupil who has not turned in his permission slip."

"I'm sure it's in here, Ms. Adolf," I said, practically diving headfirst into my backpack.

Ms. Adolf folded her arms across her gray shirt. She tapped her foot impatiently. She was wearing gray shoes with a gray buckle on them. Gray is her favorite color. That's because it goes so nicely with her gray face.

"I'm waiting," Ms. Adolf said. As if the whole class hadn't noticed.

Wow, this was a lot of pressure. Everyone in the class stared at me, except Luke Whitman, that is, who was scratching a rash on his arm with one of his vocabulary flash cards.

I pulled out a crumpled paper from the bottom of my backpack. At first, I thought it was the permission slip. But when I uncrumpled it, I saw that it was last week's math quiz, the one with the big red C-minus on top.

Tap, tap, tap. Ms. Adolf's feet were going faster. She was getting pretty mad.

The zipper pouch! That's it. I bet I stuffed the permission slip in my zipper pouch.

I pulled my head out of the bag and said, "I think I know where it is!" Then I dove back in.

I dug around in the zipper pouch and finally pulled out a half-eaten granola bar. It had a clump of greenish lint from the bottom of my backpack hanging off of it. You're probably thinking it's gross to have a linty, old granola bar crammed in your backpack, but if you saw the kind of granola bar my mom gives me for snack, trust me, you'd stuff it in your zipper pouch too. My mom doesn't believe in granola bars that have chocolate chips and marshmallows and fun stuff in them. That would be the kind that taste good. She gives me what she calls health-nola bars. That would be the kind that taste like brown construction paper.

Tap, tap, tap. Ms. Adolf's feet were certainly getting a workout. Now she was getting those red splotches on her neck too. They start appearing when I'm late or if anybody laughs in class.

"Mr. Zipzer, all permission slips were due no later than this morning," she said.

Uh-oh. It's bad enough that Ms. Adolf calls me Henry. Now it was Mr. Zipzer!

This called for extreme action. I turned my entire backpack upside down and dumped everything out on my desk. A whole bunch of crumbs and broken pencil stubs and Snapple tops and a pink high bounce came tumbling out. It wasn't a pretty sight. Worst of all, there was no permission slip anywhere.

Ms. Adolf shook her head.

"I told you yesterday, Henry, that if I did not have your signed permission slip this morning, you would not be allowed to go on the field trip tonight."

"NO!" I shouted. Whoops. I meant to say that to myself. *She wouldn't make me miss this field trip, would she?*

There are some field trips I wouldn't mind missing. Like the one in second grade when we took the bus to the pumpkin patch and Luke Whitman got carsick and threw up all over my new Converse high-tops. I could've missed that.

But tonight's field trip wasn't just any old one. It was the coolest one ever. Our entire fourth-grade class was going to spend the night on *The Pilgrim Spirit*, a tall sailing ship that was docked in New York Harbor. And that's not all. We were going to sleep over on the ship and live just like the sailors of long ago did. That means we were going to do neat things like stand watch and tie knots and sing sea songs with the captain and crew.

And now Ms. Adolf was telling me that I couldn't go? No way.

"Ms. Adolf, this isn't fair," I said.

"It's a school rule, and we cannot just break it any old time we choose," she said. "We cannot let you go on a field trip without your parents' permission, Henry. That's final."

"But my dad signed the permission slip this morning," I said. "Just before he left for his crossword puzzle convention. In green ink!"

Another blast of bad breath came flying across the room and hit me in the face like a stinky ball of burning rubber.

"A crossword puzzle convention!" Nick the Tick hooted. "Could your family be any nerdier?"

I have to confess, my family is what some people might call nerdy. Like my sister Emily has a pet iguana named Katherine and they both like to eat sardines. And my dad loves to do crossword puzzles in his boxer shorts at the end of the dining room table we don't eat on. He's a crossword puzzle nut. I mean, he'll wake up in the middle of the night just to write down a seven-letter word for monkey fur. And my mom, all you need to know about her is that her favorite thing to cook is wheatgrass noodle casserole with blueberry flecks. And then there's our dog, Cheerio. When he's not spinning in circles, he likes to lick the bricks on the fireplace just for fun.

But me thinking my family is a little on the nerdy side is a whole lot different than Nick the Tick mouthing off about it. He wasn't getting away with this.

"For your information, McKelty," I said, turning around to face him. "My dad once finished an entire *New York Times* crossword puzzle in four minutes and thirty-seven seconds. That's a tri-county record."

"Big deal," snorted McKelty. "My dad once shook hands with the king of Ethiopia."

"Like that has anything to do with anything," piped up Ashley Wong, my other best friend, who was sitting across the aisle from me.

Ashley hates it when McKelty brags, especially since most of what he says isn't true, anyway. Like in this case, maybe Nick McKelty saw a map of Ethiopia once. Suddenly, he makes it seem like his dad is best friends with the king. We call this the McKelty Factor—truth times a hundred.

Ashley went over to McKelty's desk. Even though he's huge and she's little and wears glasses, Ashley's not afraid of McKelty. She says he's all hot air. Rotting food, bad-smelling hot air, I might add. Don't his parents encourage him to brush?

I'm not sure exactly what Ashley was planning to do, but Ms. Adolf didn't like the look of things and hurried over to settle the argument. That gave Frankie a chance to talk to me.

"Take a deep breath, Zip, and fill your brain with oxygen," he said.

Frankie's mom is a yoga teacher. She's so flexible, she can touch the back of her head with the tips of her toes. She's been telling us since we were little that oxygen is brain food. I took a deep breath, in through my nose and out through my mouth, just like Frankie's mom had taught us.

"Now think, Zippola," Frankie went on,

"because your field trip future depends on this. What did you do with the permission slip?"

I played back the morning in my mind, like rewinding a tape from Blockbuster.

"I got out of bed and took a really long pee."

"Nix the yucky details," said Frankie.

"I got a pen. Got the permission slip from my three-ring binder."

"Now you're talking," Frankie nodded. "Then what?"

"Took the permission slip to my dad. Had him sign it. Put it on the hall table under the Chinese vase. Got dressed. Put on my green jacket. Kissed my mom good-bye. Grabbed my backpack. Ran out of the house."

"And forgot the permission slip under the Chinese vase," said Frankie.

Bingo!

There it was.

At least I knew the location of the permission slip. Now all I had to do was get it—immediately, if not sooner!

TEN CREATIVE WAYS TO GET THE PERMISSION SLIP YOU LEFT UNDER THE CHINESE VASE AT HOME

1. I could go to the office, get a new permission slip, and sign my father's name on the parent signature line.

2. Then I could go to jail for the rest of my life for doing that. I think maybe I'll cancel number one.

3. I'll teleport myself right into my living room, get the permission slip, and beam myself back to my seat before anyone knows I was gone.

4. Before I do that, I'll have to invent the Time Travel Teleportation Body Mover Machine.

5. I'll pretend to have a horrible stomach-ache so the school will call an ambu-lance to take me to the hospital. I'll ask the driver to swing by my apartment so I can pick up the slip.

6. I could call Permission Slips R Us. Hey, maybe it exists. You never know.

7. I could pretend to be Mr. Sicilian, the other fourth-grade teacher, and walk right out the teachers' entrance. Oops, I'd have to grow a mustache first.

8. I'll learn to talk dog talk, call Cheerio, and ask him to bring the permission slip to school. *Hey, boy, arf, arf, bow wow, ruff ruff.* Sounds right to me.

9. Hank, face it, you're not going. You're going to miss the best field trip of your entire childhood.

10. NO! I'm not giving up . . . not yet, any-way.

CHAPTER 3

It took my very best talking, but I finally convinced Ms. Adolf to give me another hour to get my signed permission slip to her. Since my dad was in New Jersey for most of the day, my only hope was to call my mom at work and ask her to bring the permission slip to school. A lot of moms would get really mad about having to leave work and come to school for something like that, but I knew my mom wouldn't. She's used to me forgetting things. She knows it's not really my fault. It's the way my brain works, or doesn't work, in this case.

Ms. Adolf gave me permission to go to the office to use the phone. The office at PS 87 is down on the first floor, past the kindergarten rooms and all the way at the end of the hall. Ms. Adolf said I had to be back in five minutes because she had a surprise waiting for us. I had no choice but to run all the way to the office.

As I ran through the halls, I kept my ears open for the sound of Principal Love's footsteps. He walks around the halls wearing these black Velcro tennis shoes, and you can hear them squeaking on the linoleum when he walks. If Principal Love sees you running in the halls, he'll either give you detention or a big old safety lecture like, "Running can lead to hurting or breaking your body." I don't know which is worse, detention or the lecture.

Luckily, the only grown-up I saw on the way to the office was Mr. Rock, who's our music teacher and maybe the coolest teacher I know. When he saw me speeding down the hall, all he said was, "Whoa, Hank, got a train to catch?"

"No, but I'm going to miss my boat if I don't hurry," I said as I whizzed past him.

Mr. Rock looked a little confused, but I didn't have time to explain.

Finally, I reached the office. Mrs. Crock, the attendance person, was at her desk eating a green salad. She always eats salad, even for breakfast. She says it's because she's on a diet, although I don't know why. I think she looks nice just the way she is.

"Hello, Hank," she said. "Have you been sent to see Principal Love again?"

"Not this time," I answered proudly.

It's not like I get sent to the principal's office every day. Let's just say I get sent there often enough that Mrs. Crock knows my parents' phone number by heart. At the beginning of fourth grade, I was sent to Principal Love's office so many times that the chair in his office was actually starting to take on the shape of my butt. But then our school psychologist Dr. Berger figured out that I have learning challenges and started giving me some special help. Now I don't get sent to the principal's office nearly as much.

"How can I help you?" Mrs. Crock asked with a smile.

I noticed that there was a leafy green piece of lettuce stuck between her front teeth. It was hard not to notice, since it covered one whole tooth and half of the other one. It's tough to decide whether you should tell a grown-up that they have something stuck in their teeth. Papa Pete, my grandfather, has a big, fluffy mustache that he calls his handlebars. We have a deal that

I always have to tell him when there's anything hanging off of it. On Saturday mornings, he likes to have crumb doughnuts with his coffee and, boy, do those things leave a trail in his mustache. Trust me, crumb doughnuts aren't called "crumb" for nothing.

I decided I didn't really know Mrs. Crock well enough to bring up the lettuce in her teeth.

"Can I use the telephone to call my mom?" I asked Mrs. Crock.

"Of course, honey," she said, smiling again. I just couldn't keep my eyes away from her lettuce . . . I mean . . . tooth. It was just smiling out at me, leafier and greener than before. I thought I saw it wave hello.

She handed me the phone and I dialed my mom's number. My mom runs the Crunchy Pickle, which is our deli on the Upper West Side of Manhattan. Papa Pete started it a long time ago, and recently turned it over to my mom when he retired. It has the best sandwiches in New York City, except (and I mean this in the nicest way) for the food my mom makes. She's always trying to invent a new kind of healthy deli food. Yummy treats like tofu-salami and chickenless chicken salad. Her food experiments may be healthy, but they have a long way to go in the taste department.

"Buenas dias, the Crunchy Pickle," said a voice on the other end of the phone. It was Carlos, my mom's number one sandwich-maker. He's my pal. Sometimes after work, we go to the park and he teaches me how to throw a curveball.

"Hi, Carlos," I said. "Is my mom there?"

"Hankito," he answered. "How's my little man?"

"I'm good," I said, "but I need to talk to my mom in a hurry."

"Oh, Hankito, she's not in the house."

"Carlos, I gotta talk to her. Can you find her?"

"No can do, little man. She's in Queens doing Mrs. Gristediano's birthday party. Three kinds of sandwiches. Roast beef, tuna, and liverwurst. She's trying to sneak in her potato free potato salad made with mung beans, but I don't think it's going to fly."

"Excuse me, Carlos." I hoped it wasn't rude to interrupt him, but by the time he finished with the menu, Ms. Adolf would have crossed me off the field trip list forever. "This is an emergency," I explained.

"An emergency!" Carlos said, sounding concerned. "You stay right where you are. I'm there and I'm taking you to the doc."

"No, Carlos. It's not a hospital kind of an emergency. It's a permission slip kind of emergency."

"Wow, that's way better," said Carlos. "Your mamacita, she can take care of that when she gets back. She'll be here at three o'clock. Well, knowing her, maybe four."

This was bad news. I only had an hour to turn in my permission slip. After that, it was over. Finito, as Carlos would say.

I couldn't call my mom and ask her to leave the party. Why should Mrs. Gristediano have her whole birthday messed up just because I'm the king of the forgetters?

"Thanks anyway, Carlos," I said.

"Call back, three o'clock. Maybe four."

That was going to be too late. It looked like the boat was sailing without me.

CHAPTER 4

I got back to class just in time to hear Ms. Adolf say my least favorite sentence in the English language.

"Pupils, take out a piece of paper and number it from one to ten."

In my experience, nothing fun ever comes after that sentence. Was I ever right, because the next thing out of her mouth went a little something like this:

"You are about to take a social studies pop quiz."

So that was the surprise Ms. Adolf had prepared for us. Wow, does she know how to have fun or what?

"For this quiz, I will read ten words out loud," Ms. Adolf droned on. "You will write the correct definition for each. Spelling counts. The first word is *dinghy*."

We had been studying nautical vocabulary to get ready for our field trip to the ship. Nautical vocabulary includes only words that have to do with ships and sailing and the seas and stuff like that. Ms. Adolf said that when we go on *The Pilgrim Spirit*, the captain and crew were going to talk to us like we were real sailors. We have to know the nautical vocabulary if we want to understand them and talk back.

"Dinghy," she repeated.

Dinghy. Think, Hank.

I remember reviewing that word, but I couldn't remember what it meant. All I could think about was that sometimes I'm a little *dingy* when I forget to focus. Man, did I not like my brain right now.

Come on, brainster. Do something.

My brain wasn't cooperating. It was thinking that everyone else was going on the field trip except me.

Dinghy. It sounds like the noise a bell makes when it rings. Dinghy. Dongy.

I was pretty sure that wasn't the right definition, so I left number one blank.

"Aft," she said.

Yes! I knew that! Sailors don't talk about the *front* or *back* of a ship, they say *fore* and *aft*. I wrote my definition. "The rear end of a ship." Ordinarily, I might have laughed at the words "rear end" because they remind me of a human butt. But I was feeling so bad about the permission slip that the idea of laughing was very far from my mind.

"Starboard," Ms. Adolf said, continuing on with the quiz.

Okay, I sort of knew that. I remembered that sailors call one side of the ship the *starboard* side and the opposite side is called *port*. But which one was the left side and which one was the right? Oh, boy. I have trouble telling left from right, no matter what you call them. You could call them *flibbery-do* and *flibbery-dee*, and I'd still be confused. Dr. Berger has told me kids with learning challenges sometimes have a hard time telling left from right—that makes me feel better. The only way I can tell for sure is to check my fingers, because the pinky finger on my left hand is a little shorter than the one on my right.

"Starboard," Ms. Adolf repeated.

I looked down at my hands. Which pinky finger was the starboard one? I didn't know.

I was so relieved when the quiz was over and the recess bell rang. Ashley and Frankie were all over me before I even had time to get my jacket on.

"Hank, what are you going to do?" Ashley asked as we headed down the stairs to the school yard. "You absolutely positively have to go on this field trip."

"She's right," Frankie agreed. "I've heard that it's more awesome than awesome."

"Rub it in," I said as we ran down the stairs.

Nick McKelty pushed past us, almost knocking both Frankie and me into the railing.

"Watch it, McKelty," said Frankie. "Stay out of my house."

"Got to get by," said Nick the Tick. "Can't you see the girls are expecting me to walk with them?"

Katie Sperling and Kim Paulson, only the two most beautiful girls in the fourth grade, were a few stairs ahead of us. I'm sure the last thing they wanted was to have Mr. Bad Breath panting along next to them.

"Watch," said Ashley. "As soon as they get a whiff of him, they're going to duck into the girls' bathroom."

McKelty shoved his way up to Katie and Kim and gave them a big smile. I couldn't hear what he said, but I could see both of them back away from his fishy breath. I bet the smell fried the ends of their hair. Just as Ashley predicted, when Katie and Kim got to the hall, they immediately ducked into the girls' bathroom.

"Nice call, Ashweena," Frankie said.

I pushed open the double door to the school yard and we went outside. Even though it was officially spring and there were little green leaves on all the trees, it was still pretty cold. As we stopped to zip up our jackets, McKelty appeared again.

"You bring any of those yummy Twinkies in your lunch today?" he asked Ashley. McKelty always comes by our table at lunch and tries to swipe Ashley's dessert. He's a total Twinkie hog.

"What's it to you?" answered Ashley, snapping her head around so her ponytail flipped in his face. "You won't be having any."

"We'll see about that," he said. A basketball

came bouncing toward him. *Bonk!* It hit him on the head and bounced off. The big lug didn't even react.

"Nice reflexes," Frankie said.

"Oh yeah?" McKelty shot back.

"Nice comeback too," Ashley added.

The conversation was moving too fast for McKelty and he stomped off to join the basketball game. Ordinarily, Frankie would have been the first one on the court. He's got the best moves of any kid in our class. He can stuff it from the inside, and from the outside it's nothing but net. But he said no when Ryan Shimozato asked him to join his team. Ashley stayed back too. I'm lucky to have such good friends, the kind that won't just go off and shoot baskets when I have a problem.

Ashley pushed her glasses back on her nose and started twirling her ponytail, which she does when she's thinking hard.

"Operation permission slip," she said. She was all business. "Let's come up with a plan. The way I see it, gentlemen, we have forty-five minutes." She checked her watch, which was decorated with blue and lavender rhinestones.

Ashley glues rhinestones onto all her clothes, so when you see her in the sunlight, she's very sparkly.

It was quiet. Too quiet.

"All ideas are welcome," Frankie said. "Speak right up."

I couldn't think of anything. My dad was in New Jersey. My mom was in Queens. My dachshund Cheerio was spinning in a circle. And the permission slip was at home with him. End of story.

Ashley kept twirling her ponytail.

"Come on, guys," she said. "Where there's a will, there's a way. Isn't that what Papa Pete always says?"

Bam! There it was. Papa Pete!

You know how when you've been friends with people for a really long time, sometimes you get the exact same idea at the exact same time? Well, that's what happened.

"If I'm not mistaken, I believe Papa Pete has a key to your apartment," Ashley said.

"That he does," I answered with a big grin.

"Gentlemen, we have our plan," said Ashley.

CHAPTER 5

We ran to the office faster than you can say, "Hank Daniel Zipzer, you're going on the field trip, after all!" Go ahead, try saying it. Now you know exactly how long it took us to get there. Pretty fast, huh?

Mrs. Crock was at her desk. She smiled at us. Yup, you guessed it. Old Mr. Lettuce Leaf was still there. I looked away, but Frankie didn't.

"If you don't mind my saying so, Mrs. Crock, you have something large and green playing hooky on your teeth," Frankie said without batting an eye. Then he flashed her that big grin, the one that makes the dimple pop in on his left cheek.

"Thank you for pointing that out, Frankie dear," said Mrs. Crock. Then she reached in her drawer, got out her mirror, pulled the piece of lettuce off her tooth, and sent it on its merry way to the wastebasket.

See, that's the difference between Frankie Townsend and me. I spent five whole minutes wondering if I should say anything to Mrs. Crock, but Frankie, he just broke the news like it was nothing. That's called confidence, and it's what you have when you're good at everything like Frankie is.

"May we use the telephone?" Ashley asked Mrs. Crock. "Hank has to call his grandfather because he forgot his permission slip."

"Certainly, Ashley dear," said Mrs. Crock.

And that's the difference between Ashley Wong and me. She knows exactly what she wants and isn't afraid to ask for it. Boom, just like that. From her brain to her mouth, out it comes.

Ashley picked up the phone. "What's Papa Pete's number at home?" she asked me.

"He's not there," I said. "He bowls Tuesday and Thursday mornings."

Papa Pete is the best senior bowler on the Upper West Side. His team, the Chopped Livers, has won the league championship at McKelty's Roll 'N Bowl for three years in a row. A long time ago, when he was in the navy, Papa Pete bowled a 300. In case you're not up on your bowling statistics, that is a perfect game. He never brags about it, though. I just happened to see the scorecard once when we were looking at pictures in his old photo album.

"I'll go ask Nick the Tick what the phone number is at his dad's bowling alley," said Ashley.

Nick McKelty's father owns the bowling alley on 86th Street where Papa Pete bowls. That's why it's called McKelty's Roll 'N Bowl.

"Forget that creep," Frankie said. "We'll find the number ourselves. Mrs. Crock, can we borrow your phone book?"

"Certainly, dear," she said, smiling. Her teeth were as white as those little baby marshmallows that you float in your hot chocolate.

Mrs. Crock got the phone book from her drawer and handed it to me. I flipped it open to the M's and looked at the page. It seemed to me like there were a million little gray letters swimming around on that page like tadpoles in a pond. I could feel my eyes crossing.

In case I haven't mentioned it, I'm not too

good at spelling. You might even say I stink at spelling. Ditto for reading. Double ditto for alphabetizing. Put all that together, and what you get is that looking up a name in the phone book is not my idea of a good time. And don't even talk to me about dictionaries. How can you look up a word that you don't know how to spell in the first place, or even know how to sound out? I'm still waiting for someone to explain that to me.

Frankie has known me my whole life, so he knew that if I looked up the phone number, we could have been there until next Easter, or maybe even summer.

"Mind if I have a look, Zip?" he said, taking the phone book out of my hands. He flipped through the pages and found the number easily. Ashley dialed it, and handed the phone to me. We're a good team, the three of us.

"McKelty's Roll 'N Bowl," answered Mr. McKelty in a friendly voice. I wondered how such a nice man could produce such a jerky kid.

"Hello, Mr. McKelty. This is Hank Zipzer," I said. "Is my grandfather there?"

"Is he here?" he shouted. "Son, he just

bowled four strikes in a row. He's here and he's hot. Hang on, and I'll try to pry him off the lane."

I could hear all the bowling alley sounds through the phone as I waited for Papa Pete to pick up. The balls rolling down the oiled wooden lanes, the pins clattering as they fell over, Fern the waitress calling out orders in the coffee shop. That Fern, she makes an excellent root-beer float. If you're ever in the neighborhood, check it out.

"Hankie, my boy. What'd you forget?" It was the first thing Papa Pete said when he picked up the phone, before he even said hello.

"How'd you know?" I asked him.

"Grandfathers know these things," he said. "It's our job."

Wow, he was amazing.

"I left my permission slip for tonight's field trip under the Chinese vase," I said. "They won't let me go unless I turn it in."

"When do you need it?"

"Ten minutes ago."

"Ten minutes ago, it is," said Papa Pete. "I'll jog over to your apartment lickety-split and be at school in two shakes of a lamb's tail. Meet me in the lobby by the trophy case."

"Papa Pete, I'm sorry you have to leave," I said. "I hear you're on a hot streak."

"Hot, schmot," said Papa Pete. "Bowling's a game. You're my grandson. Be right there, Hankie."

Click. Before he even said good-bye, he was gone.

Do I have the best grandfather in the world? Let me answer that for you.

Yes, I do.

CHAPTER 6

Frankie and Ashley went back to our classroom to tell Ms. Adolf that I would be a few minutes late getting back to class. I waited by the trophy case for Papa Pete.

The walls all around the lobby were covered with kindergarten art. I guess you'd call it art. There were about fifty pieces of colored paper taped to the wall, each one with a green leaf glued in the middle. The theme was springtime. I went and looked at one of the leaves close-up. When I got near enough to the paper, I could smell the white glue, the kind we used in kindergarten. I loved school then. No spelling tests, no pop social studies quizzes, no homework, no pressure. Just building with blocks and dressing up like firefighters and gluing a piece of noodle on colored paper. Man, I was a whiz with glue.

Finally, the front door burst open and Papa

Pete came running in. He was wearing his red sweats, and he looked like a giant strawberry. A giant sweating strawberry. You've got to hand it to him, though. He jogged all the way there, which is pretty good for a guy who's going to be sixty-eight on June 26.

"Hankie, I got something you're going to love," Papa Pete said with a big grin.

"My permission slip?" I asked.

"Sure, sure, I got that," he said, handing me the blue slip of paper. "But look what else I brought."

He handed me a ziplock baggie. It had a pickle inside.

"Your mother happened to have a couple of dills in the fridge. I thought you might want a snack."

Papa Pete and I love to eat pickles together. Sometimes, he stops at the Crunchy Pickle and picks up whatever is fresh—half dills, garlic rounds, bread and butters—and we sit on the balcony outside my living room and eat them.

"Thanks, Papa Pete," I said. "It looks great, but I've got to get the permission slip to my teacher now. I'm really late."

"You go," Papa Pete said. "And don't worry. I'll save the pickle for after school and—"

He was interrupted by a sound I've never heard coming from Papa Pete. It was a cell phone playing "Take Me Out to the Ballgame." Papa Pete reached into his pocket and took out a brand-new, shiny, silver phone.

"Papa Pete!" I said. "When did you get a cell phone?"

"Yesterday!" he said. "Do you know you can play games on this thing? And check the baseball scores?"

Papa Pete reached out and pinched my cheek, like he always does.

"I love this cheek and everything attached to it," he said. Then he turned to leave. I could see him pressing buttons on his cell phone like crazy and saying, "Hello, is someone there?" as he disappeared out the door.

I looked at the clock in the hall. I had three minutes to get to class and turn in my slip. I did my super-speed walk down the hall to the stairway.

Squeak, squeak, squeak. Oh, no. Principal Love's Velcro shoes were coming down the hall from the opposite direction. And he was in them! Just my luck.

"Well, young Mr. Zipzer," Principal Love said in a booming voice. "What are you doing in the halls during class time?"

Principal Love has this mole on his cheek that Frankie and I swear looks just like the Statue of Liberty, but without the torch. When he talks, he sounds like he should be tall with bushy black hair, but actually he's short and mostly bald.

"Nothing, sir," I said. My voice sounded really little.

"Nothing accomplishes nothing, which is nothing you can use the next time you need it," he said, holding one finger in the air like he had just said something really important. "Remember that, Young Zipzer."

"Yes, sir, I will," I squeaked. "I have to go now."

"First, I have something of extreme importance to tell you," Principal Love said, getting so close to my face that I thought I could see eyes on his Statue of Liberty mole.

Oh, no. Here comes one of his lectures.

I have never understood one thing Principal Love says when he lectures me. And the most annoying thing is he says everything twice, which means I don't understand it twice in a row.

"The greatest accomplishments are put into effect by doing something," he said. "That's what I always tell young people. Yes, indeed. The greatest accomplishments are put into effect by doing something."

"I'll never forget that, sir," I said. "Thank you, but I have to get my permission slip to Ms. Adolf now."

I looked up at the clock on the wall. I had one-and-a-half minutes left. I really had to go, but Principal Love looked like he had more to say. *Please let him be finished,* I thought. Then a lucky thing happened. Phillip Gunning, a huge fifth-grader with size-twelve Nikes, came running down the stairs at breakneck speed.

"Mr. Gunning," Principal Love said in his bushy-haired man voice. "There is no running in these halls. Approach me immediately."

That was my chance. I said a silent good-bye to the Statue of Liberty mole and started up the stairs as fast as I could go without running. I could hear Principal Love beginning to lecture Phillip Gunning, but I never looked back.

My class had already started science when I came bursting in.

"Here, Ms. Adolf," I said, waving my blue permission slip at her. "I've got it."

Ms. Adolf looked at the clock, then at me.

"You're late," she said. "It's thirty seconds past the hour."

Oh, no. She wasn't going to keep me from going because I was thirty seconds late. She wouldn't do that. Not even Ms. Adolf would do that.

"Please, Ms. Adolf," I said, thrusting the permission slip practically in her face. "I did my super-speed walk all the way here, even though I have a big blister on my left heel and really shouldn't be speed-walking at this moment in time. And, besides, Principal Love stopped me in the hall."

Ms. Adolf took the permission slip and looked it over. My heart was beating fast. I glanced over at Frankie and Ashley. They looked like they were hardly breathing.

"All right, Henry. I'll make an exception this time," she said.

"Does that mean I can go on the field trip?" I asked.

"Yes, Henry. You may go."

"Thank you, Ms. Adolf! Thank you so much!"

I was so happy, I could have hugged her. Wait. I take the hugging part back. But I was really happy.

To my complete shock, everyone in the class burst into applause.

"Way to go, Hank," all my friends said. Wow, that made me feel really good.

CHAPTER 7

I don't know if you've ever been in New York City at Christmastime, but it's unbelievable. The best thing about it is that everybody's in a great mood. Just walking down the street looking at the decorated store windows and watching the snow fall makes everybody happy. No one in the whole city is mean or grumpy.

Well, that's the way it felt that day in Ms. Adolf's class. We were all so happy to be going on *The Pilgrim Spirit* and so excited about the trip, that no one was mean or grumpy. And, yes, that included Nick McKelty. The big lug actually turned nice.

In the afternoon, we were discussing all the jobs kids were going to be assigned on the ship. Some people were going to be on the cleaning crew or on the ropes crew. Some were going to be line handlers. Other kids were going to work in the galley, which is what they call a kitchen on a ship.

Nick McKelty said that his big brother Joseph had been on *The Pilgrim Spirit* three years before, and he thought the most fun job was the captain's assistant. The captain's assistant got to accompany the captain on his rounds and help give orders. That sounded so cool. I could see myself doing that.

Just to show you how good a mood everyone was in, during our class discussion, Nick actually suggested that I should be the captain's assistant. He said he thought I deserved it since I almost didn't get to go. At first, I thought I was hearing things. I mean, ever since we were in preschool, Nick McKelty had only said mean things to me.

"What's up with you, McKelty?" I whispered to him.

"Can't a guy do something nice every once in a while?" he said. "I feel sorry for you, Zipzer. You had a rough morning."

Hey, I'd take his pity, if it meant I'd get to be captain's assistant. I'm not too big for that.

The class took a vote and I got the job.

Only one person voted against me, and believe it or not, it wasn't Nick McKelty. It was Luke Whitman, who felt that he deserved the job more because he owned a real pirate hat with a big feather. When Ms. Adolf explained that *The Pilgrim Spirit* wasn't a pirate ship, Luke changed his mind and voted for me. He said he only wanted to be a captain's assistant on a pirate ship, anyway.

This was too good to be true. I was spending the night on *The Pilgrim Spirit* and I was going to be the captain's assistant.

Some days start out bad, and just wind up perfect.

CHAPTER 8

School was out at three o'clock, but we had to be back by five o'clock sharp with our bags. It would take us about a half hour by school bus to reach the South Street Seaport where *The Pilgrim Spirit* was docked. Even though we weren't scheduled to go on board until six, we had to leave time for New York City traffic. Once we were aboard the ship, we'd be under the command of the captain until nine-thirty the next morning, when our parents were coming to pick us up at the dock.

I had a lot to do to get ready, so I was nervous when Frankie's dad didn't show up exactly at three o'clock to walk us home.

There were five of us waiting in front of the school. Frankie, Ashley, and I all live in the same apartment building on 78th Street. We always walk to and from school together. Then there was my sister Emily, who unfortunately lives in the same apartment as I do.

The fifth person was the supremely annoying Robert Upchurch, the biggest third-grade nuisance that ever tried to breathe. I say tried because his nasal passages are always clogged with mucus. My sister Emily's nasal passages are in the same clogged condition, so the two of them have bonded, nasally speaking. Robert hangs out with us a lot, because my mom says it's not polite to leave him out since he lives in the building too.

Robert is the kind of kid who wears a white shirt and tie to school just because he feels like it. He's not even in the orchestra or anything. Lately, we've gotten lucky because Robert has been spending a lot of time with Emily. They share a deep interest in iguanas and geckos and snakes and many other nerdish things.

Frankie's dad arrived a few minutes after three. It's only a few blocks to our building, but he set out at a really fast pace. We had to take four steps for each one of his.

Dr. Townsend is a professor at Columbia University and he uses so many big words that I have trouble following what he's saying. As we walked, he talked a lot about our field trip that night. Even though he teaches African-American Studies, he seemed to know a bunch about sailing ships.

"I hear that *The Pilgrim Spirit* is a precise replica of the brig that Richard Henry Dana sailed," he said as we passed Kim's Grocery. I could smell all the flowers in their buckets of water lining the front of the store.

"What's a brig?" I asked. "And while we're at it, could you tell me what a replica is too?"

"A replica means that the ship you're staying on is an exact copy of Dana's original," Dr. Townsend said. "And a brig is a type of ship."

"Actually, a brig is a two-masted vessel with square sails on both masts," piped up Robert. "And a secondary definition is that it is a military jail."

Dr. Townsend looked very surprised that Robert would know something like that. The rest of us weren't surprised. We have to listen to Robert all the time, and he's like a walking encyclopedia of useless information. Without asking, he will tell you the main crop of Outer

Mongolia, besides rocks. Every time he opens his mouth, something boring leaks out.

"Was Richard Henry Dana a pirate?" Emily asked. "I'd like to be a pirate."

"Oh yeah, you'd look a lot better with an eye patch," I said.

She wrinkled up her nose at me, and I wrinkled up mine back at her. Two can play that game.

"Richard Henry Dana was a writer," said Dr. Townsend. "He authored the classic book *Two Years Before the Mast*. It described what life was like on a merchant sailing ship almost two hundred years ago."

"Actually, his book was published in 1840," Robert said.

"How do you know that, Robert?" Dr. Townsend asked. I couldn't tell if he was impressed or annoyed. As for me, I was in the annoyed category.

"I read all about *The Pilgrim Spirit* during library period today," said Robert. "I have many more facts I'd be happy to share with you."

"Thanks, dude, but my ears are closed for

business right now," Frankie said.

"When do they reopen?" the clueless one asked.

"Uh . . . when we get back from our seafaring," Frankie said.

"Besides, we won't be able to hear you over the traffic," Ashley added.

"Good one, Ashweena," Frankie whispered to her.

"I'd love to hear what you learned," my sister Emily piped up. See what I mean about Emily and Robert sharing an interest in super nerdy things? There was no turning off Robert now. And, believe me, I looked for the switch.

"Richard Henry Dana's ship set sail from Boston and sailed around Cape Horn, which is the tip of South America," said Robert.

"Everybody knows what Cape Horn is, dude," Frankie snapped.

Everyone but me. I didn't know. So I kept my mouth shut.

"The ship picked up animal hides in California," Robert droned on. "Then it sailed all the way back to Boston where the hides were made into shoes and other leather goods."

"I don't believe in making shoes from the skins of animals," said Emily. "Just think of my beautiful Katherine, made into a pair of shoes."

"You don't have to worry about her," I said. "Katherine's too ugly to be made into anything. Who'd want a pair of scaly, gray shoes with a long, snapping tongue?"

"That's not funny, Hank," said Emily. "I happen to love Katherine."

"Sorry, Em," I said. "I hope Katherine lives a long and happy life. Just not in my bathtub."

Hey, I know what I'm saying. She loves to poop in there. Katherine, not Emily, that is.

With Dr. Townsend setting the pace and all of us running away from Robert, we reached our apartment building in world-record time. As we approached the front door, we ran into Papa Pete and my mom. They were just coming up the street from the other direction. I could tell that my mom had been working all day, because she was wearing one of her big headbands. She puts them on to keep her curly hair out of her face so it doesn't get all crusty with her food experiments. Before she discovered that trick, she always used to have little chunks of soylami or mock tuna in her hair at the end of the day.

"Hi, everyone," my mom said. "Big night tonight, huh?"

Then she sang, "Yo ho, yo ho, a pirate's life for me." My mom has a song for every occasion.

She rubbed me on the head as I held the door open for her. I wondered if Carlos had told her about my phone call.

"How're my grandkids?" Papa Pete said, giving each of us a pinch on the cheek as we walked by him into the lobby area. Papa Pete wasn't just talking about me and Emily. He calls Frankie and Ashley his grandkids too, because he likes them so much. I can't imagine he feels that way about Robert, but Papa Pete would never leave him out. He even gave his bony little face a pinch. Ick and double ick.

As I pressed the button for the elevator, Ashley checked her watch.

"It's three-thirty," she said. "We have to be at the bus at five. That gives us an hour-and-a-half to pack, snack, and get back to school."

"Hank," my mom said. "Be sure you remember to pack your sleeping bag."

"I will, Mom."

"In fact, before we leave for school, I want to check your duffel bag to make sure you have it."

"You don't have to do that, Mom," I said.

"You know how you always forget things," Emily said to me. "You're such a brainless one." I really didn't feel like letting her get away with that.

"Oh really, Emily? Tell me, when was the last time I forgot something?"

I looked over at Papa Pete, but he said nothing. He just kept looking at the numbers above the elevator. Frankie and Ashley did the same.

"Okay, I take it back," Emily said.

"Good."

It wasn't until we were inside the elevator, tucked against the back wall, that Papa Pete looked over at me and winked.

CHAPTER 9

"**Mom, do you know** where my Mets sweat-shirt is?" I hollered from my bedroom.

I must have yelled a little too loud, because I startled Cheerio, who was sleeping under-neath my desk. He jumped up and started to spin around, chasing his tail like crazy, and spun himself right out of my room. He moves pretty fast, considering that he's going in circles.

"Your sweatshirt should be in your bottom drawer, where it always is," my mom hollered back from the kitchen.

I had already pulled everything out of my bottom drawer. My Mets sweatshirt was miss-ing. It was the one thing I really wanted to take on the overnight on *The Pilgrim Spirit*. It made me feel warm, both inside and out. If you couldn't tell, I'm a major New York Mets fan.

"I can't believe it! It's not here, Mom," I yelled.

My dad appeared at the door of my room. He was in an excellent mood, having come in second in the All New Jersey Crossword Puzzle Competition. Apparently, he was the only one who had known that a "plover" was a six-letter word for a round-bodied, short-tailed wading bird. If that doesn't put a guy in a great mood, I don't know what will.

"Hank, sweatshirts don't just get up and walk away," he said.

No sooner had he said those words than I looked down and saw my sweatshirt walking away. I'm not kidding. It was heading out the door of my room and down the hall.

"Want to bet?" I said, and ran after it. By the time I reached it, it had walked right into Emily's room.

"Come back here!" I cried, grabbing the sweatshirt with both hands. As I pulled it off, underneath it was her lovely iguana, Katherine.

"Hank, what are you doing to her?" Emily wailed.

"What? What am I dong? I'm taking back

what's mine," I said. "And please tell your scaly lizoid to keep her claws out of my drawers."

"Kathy likes to snuggle up in soft clothes," Emily said. "You know that."

"Then let her curl up in your sock drawer. My Mets things are off-limits."

Emily patted Katherine on the snout. "It's okay, sweetie," she said in her baby-talk iguana voice. "Hank doesn't mean it."

"Yes, I do," I shouted. "Don't believe her, Katherine. I mean it."

The bathroom door opened and Papa Pete came out.

"What's all the commotion about?" he asked. "A man can't concentrate in there."

"Why do you have to concentrate in the bathroom?" asked Emily.

"I was reading," said Papa Pete. "For your information, young lady, a bathroom is an excellent place to catch up on fine reading material."

He held up a booklet. It was the instructions for his new cell phone.

"I tell you, Stan," he said to my dad. "I need a college degree in cell phone-ology to understand this."

Boy, I couldn't agree more. I've never been able to understand one word of any operating instructions manual. That's a problem when every single toy or electronic device you get comes with a book of instructions. Fortunately, Frankie likes to read instruction books, so he figures out how something works, then shows me how. I can work anything once I see how to do it.

"Technology," my dad said to Papa Pete. "It's a ten-letter word for the future."

Sometimes I think my dad actually thinks in crossword puzzles.

"What are you trying to learn, Papa Pete?" I asked.

"I just want to set up my voicemail on this phone. Think you can do it, Hankie?"

"Sure," I said. Frankie and I had done it on his dad's phone. "I'll take a look as soon as I finish packing."

I took his cell phone and stuffed it in the pocket of my jacket. Then I went back into my room to finish packing my duffel bag.

"Got everything?" my mom said, sticking her head in my door.

"Yup," I answered, checking off each item as I put it in. "Change of shoes. Camp pillow. Mets sweatshirt. Clean socks. Wool cap. Toothbrush. Striped toothpaste. Flashlight."

"Snack," she said, and handed me a baggie with something inside that didn't look like it belonged to any food group I know.

"What's this, Mom?"

"Tofu jerky."

"Sounds . . . uh . . . interesting."

I put it in my duffel, stuffing it way at the bottom so I would never have to see it again.

"Where's your sleeping bag?" my mom asked.

"Oops. I was just going to get it. And you thought I forgot it, didn't you?"

My mom gave me a look, but was nice enough not to say anything.

I went to my closet and dragged out my sleeping bag, the blue one with the plaid flannel inside. I had shoved it in there last weekend after Frankie slept over. I'm supposed to put it back in its stuff sack, but I can never get it back in. I don't know why they make stuff sacks so small. I mean, you have this huge puffy sleeping bag and a tiny bag it's supposed to fit in. Every time I try to stuff it in the sack, a huge clump of it is left hanging out.

My mom tried to help me, but even she had trouble. By the time we got the sleeping bag jammed in its stuff sack, my dad was in my room pointing to his watch.

"Time to go," he said. "The Townsends called and I told them to go on ahead with the Wongs."

I added the sleeping bag to my duffel, zipped it up, and dragged it out into the living room. Papa Pete gave me a hug good-bye. It's more of a lift than a hug, because my feet always leave the floor. He was staying home with Emily while we walked to school.

"Good luck, Hankie," Papa Pete said. "I wish I were going with you. I was quite a sailor in my navy days, you know. What you want to watch out for are high winds and pea soup fog. Those are dangerous conditions."

"You don't have to worry about that," I answered. "We're not even leaving the dock."

"You're not? What kind of ship is this?" he asked.

"It's a floating classroom," I said. "We're going to experience what life at sea was like in 1840, but we're not actually going out to sea."

"That sounds like an exciting way to learn," said Papa Pete.

"And guess what?" I added. "I'm the captain's assistant, which is a pretty important position."

"I'm impressed," said Papa Pete.

Papa Pete put his hand up to his forehead and saluted me.

"Well, Captain's Assistant. Anchors aweigh."

Then he pinched my cheek, like always.

As we were leaving, I bent down to say good-bye to Cheerio.

"So long, boy," I said, scratching him behind his ears. "I'm not going to see you until tomorrow."

I'm pretty sure he understood me, because he started to whimper in a way that made me so sad. Then he rolled over for me to scratch his stomach like he always does before I leave.

"Can he come?" I asked my dad. "Not on the boat, just to school."

"I guess so," my dad said. "He could use

some fresh air. I'll get his leash."

We rode down the elevator and walked up 78th Street across Amsterdam Avenue to my school. Cheerio kept stopping to sniff every little thing. The pink carnations outside of Mr. Kim's grocery store. The wheels of the hot pretzel stand on the corner. And let's not forget the old French fry he dug out of a sidewalk crack. And the fire hydrants, every single one of them. His nose was working overtime, but, boy, was he happy.

I got really excited when we got close to the school building. I saw the big yellow school bus parked in front. My whole class was there, saying good-bye to their parents and climbing on board.

Ms. Adolf was standing by the door, checking each person off in her roll book. Wow, I didn't think that book had ever been that far from the top drawer of her desk. She was wearing jeans and tennis shoes and a pink knit hat with a pom-pom on top. She looked almost normal without her all-gray outfit.

"Hello, Henry," she said. "I see you're late."

"I'm so sorry, Ms. Adolf," my mom said.

"We had trouble getting the sleeping bag in the stuff sack. I'm sure you understand."

"No, I don't," Ms. Adolf said in her usual sourpuss voice.

The thing about Cheerio is that he either likes you or doesn't like you. If he likes you, he wags his tail and nips at your ankles and makes the cutest little yipping sounds. But if he doesn't like you, he points his nose straight up in the air and starts to howl like a coyote. Then he runs in circles around you and won't stop until either he falls over or you do.

He did not like Ms. Adolf. No sir. Make that a definite dislike.

The minute he heard her voice, he stuck his nose up in the air and howled like a werewolf in a horror movie. Then he broke loose from my dad, who was holding his leash, and starting circling her like his feet were on fire.

"Can you please stop him," said Ms. Adolf. Her teeth were clenched really tight together.

My dad lunged for Cheerio's leash, but he missed. This made Cheerio run faster and howl louder. I saw Frankie and Ashley out of the corner of my eye. They were hanging out of the bus window, covering their mouths so they wouldn't laugh.

"Cheerio," I said. "Come here, boy."

Cheerio stopped and looked me right in the eye. He was thinking hard about it.

"Get this animal away from me," Ms. Adolf yelled. "We've been through this once before on the ball field."

That did it. Cheerio just does not like the sound of her voice. He howled louder than before and started circling again. Ms. Adolf tried to jump away, but her feet somehow got caught up in Cheerio's leash.

Boom! Down she went onto the sidewalk.

Rip!

What was that?

I'll tell you what it was. It was Ms. Adolf's jeans, ripping right down the rear end. It wasn't a little rip, either.

"My underpants!" she screamed. "Don't look, pupils!"

As if any of us would want to. Well, except for Luke Whitman, who reported that they were white.

My mom handed Ms. Adolf a jacket to tie

around herself. My dad grabbed Cheerio and picked him up.

"I'm so sorry, Ms. Adolf," my mom said. "I don't know what got into him."

"That's why I don't approve of pets of any kind," said Ms. Adolf. "Some people find them cute, but I find them unpredictable and much too furry."

We all had to wait on the bus while Ms. Adolf went inside and changed into different clothes. When she came out wearing her gray school skirt with tennis shoes and her pink pom-pom hat, it was all we could do not to burst out laughing.

She climbed onto the bus and the doors closed.

"South Street Seaport, next stop, driver," she said.

As we pulled away from the curb, I turned and looked out the window. My dad was holding onto Cheerio, and as the bus headlights flashed on him, I could see his little face clearly.

I could have sworn he was smiling.

CHAPTER 10

South Street Seaport is in Lower Manhattan. That's all the way downtown near the Brooklyn Bridge. Since we live on the Upper West Side, we had to travel down along the West Side Highway to reach the seaport. The traffic was terrible like it usually is in New York. Everyone was honking and taxis were cutting in and out, but we didn't care. We could hardly wait to get our first view of the tall ships.

The sky was turning gray by the time the driver stopped the bus at the seaport. We got out and walked a little ways to the Maritime Museum, which is in the center of the Seaport Village. Ms. Adolf made us stand stiff and still while she read us the plaque in front of the museum.

The sign told about the history of South Street Seaport. I don't know how interested you are, so I'll just give you the short version. In the old days of New York, it used to be a really busy harbor, so busy that they called it the Street of Ships. But when sailing ships got replaced by steamships, people stopped using the harbor, so the South Street Seaport got pretty grungy. Not too long ago, it got restored to what it is now, which is a really cool new place that looks like a really cool old place.

Ms. Adolf had to stop reading a couple of times because Luke Whitman kept talking to the seagulls. He can make this sound in his throat that I swear sounds like he's a bird. A whole bunch of seagulls were circling around us.

"Luke," Ms. Adolf finally said, "unless you'd like a flock of seagulls to do their business on your head, I suggest you stop making that sound."

Boy, that shut him up fast. Nothing like the threat of bird poop dripping down your face to straighten a guy out.

By then it was getting dark, but I could see pretty well with the light of the old street lamps. We were surrounded by winding cobblestone streets. No cars were allowed, probably to make it seem like it used to be back in the old days. I noticed that even the shops and restaurants were replicas of old buildings. Then I thought how proud Dr. Townsend would be if he knew that the word "replica" was just floating around in my brain with other normal words like "home run" and "bird poop."

We walked about two blocks down to the waterfront. Another yellow school bus was parked in the lot and a group of kids about our age was getting out.

"Watch out! Pirates!" Nick McKelty yelled.

Everybody laughed but you-know-who-with-the-pink-pom-pom-hat. After she told us to stop laughing immediately, Ms. Adolf explained that we were sharing *The Pilgrim Spirit* with a fourth-grade class from PS 9. We were supposed to show them our best manners.

Frankie tugged at the sleeve of my jacket.

"You're facing the wrong way, Zip. Check it out."

I turned around and looked toward the water. Man oh man oh man oh man. There she was, *The Pilgrim Spirit*. It was the coolest ship I had ever seen.

I'm not kidding you. *The Pilgrim Spirit* looked just like one of those old ships you see in a glass bottle, only big. I mean really big. They don't call it a tall ship for nothing. The masts were as tall as telephone poles, and the sails were the size of ten bedsheets. Ropes were strung everywhere, tied in big knots to shiny brass rings.

"He's beautiful," Ashley whispered.

"*She's* beautiful," I corrected her. We had learned that you always refer to a ship as she, even though they're not officially girls. Like you'd say, "The *Queen Mary*, she's a fine ship, that she is." I was surprised that Ashley hadn't remembered that.

"I'm not talking about the boat," Ashley said. "I'm talking about *him*."

Ashley was staring at the busload of kids from PS 9. Actually, she was staring at one boy—a tall good-looking guy with a really thick head of blond hair. She couldn't take her eyes off him.

"Ashweena, what's wrong with you?" Frankie said.

"Nothing."

"Then what are you staring at?"

"Collin Sebastian Rich the Fourth," she said.

"Do you know that dude?" Frankie asked her.

"No."

"Then how do you know his name?" I said. We had never seen Ashley like this before.

"He went to soccer camp with me. He was MVP every day."

"So the dude can kick. What's the big deal?" Frankie said.

"No big deal," Ashley said. "He's just perfect, that's all. He's really smart too."

A girl I had never seen before came running up to Ashley. They looked at each other and screamed.

"Ashley!" squealed the girl. "I haven't seen you since soccer camp!"

"Chelsea!" Ashley squealed right back. "Are you staying on the ship? This is so awesome!"

They hugged each other and jumped up and down like baseball players who had just won the World Series.

"Come meet my friends from my school," Chelsea said.

"Is he one of them?" Ashley asked, pointing to

the guy with the big head of hair.

"Collin?" said Chelsea. "He's great. Come on, I'll introduce you."

Ashley turned to Frankie and me. "Do you mind, guys?"

"Go right ahead," I said.

"Yeah, Hank and I have knots to tie and sails to trim and important stuff like that. Don't we, my man?" Frankie didn't seem too happy.

Ashley ran off with Chelsea. I could see her getting introduced to Collin. He seemed to be staring at Ashley's rhinestone hat with a sea-blue rhinestone tall ship that she had made especially for our field trip. He was smiling and looked like he had just stepped out of one of those *Teen People* magazines that are on the coffee table in my orthodontist's office.

I stared at the guy for a long minute. I thought about what it would feel like to be him instead of me. I do that sometimes.

If I were Collin Sebastian Rich the Fourth, I'd be really happy with my great head of blond hair that was perfectly cut.

Okay, Hank. Yours is dark and pretty messy, but if you put enough mousse in it, it can look decent, at least for a while.

I'd be tall and everyone would look up to me.

Okay, Hank, so you're a little on the short side. You'll grow. Maybe.

If I were Collin, I'd be a great soccer and football player. But I'd be really modest about it when I won the game every time.

Don't feel bad, Hank. You are definitely above average at archery.

My closet would be filled with Gap clothes. Yup, it'd be Gap all the way.

So what if the Zipzers don't care where they shop? My dad always says clothes are good as long as they cover the body.

Along with being great-looking and a great athlete, I'd be really smart in school.

You have dyslexia, Hank, but you can get C's if you focus, work hard, and, hey, even smart guys like Albert Einstein didn't do well in math.

Wait a minute. Can I be honest with you for a minute? As I stood there at South Street Seaport wondering what it would be like to be Collin Sebastian Rich the Fourth, I had only one thought.

I'd give anything to be him.

CHAPTER 11

Before they let us on the ship, a man from the Coast Guard came and talked to us about boat safety. He told us where the life vests were and how to signal if we were in distress and what to do in foul weather. I don't know why we had to hear all that stuff. It wasn't like we were even leaving the dock.

After he left, we waited in line to go onto the ship, which wasn't so bad because it gave me time to take a good look at *The Pilgrim Spirit.* She was painted black on the bottom, and made entirely out of wood. The sails were mostly square, except for three big triangle ones at the front and one at the back. Excuse me. I meant to say *fore* and *aft.* There was a gangway, which is a ramp, leading from the dock onto the ship.

Ms. Adolf and Mr. Lingg, who was the teacher from PS 9, got on board first. We couldn't see where they went, but someone said they went below deck where there are special quarters for the teachers.

They let the kids go on board one at a time. Just before you stepped on the deck, you had to say your name to the sailor at the top of the gangway and salute.

Ashley had gone off with Chelsea and some kids from PS 9 including Collin "Mr. Perfect" Rich. Frankie and I were among the last kids to get on board. I arranged it that way because I figured the last ones to go on were going to be closest to the front. When you're on the short side like I am, you always have to figure out how to be in front. That's one of my rules. Otherwise, you spend a lot of time looking at the back of someone's head.

Heather Payne was standing behind us as we waited to board.

"I think I'm seasick," she said.

"Heather, get it together. We're on dry land," Frankie pointed out.

"Then I think I'm landsick," she answered.

We let her go ahead of us, just in case she barfed. Never stand in front of someone who's about to barf. That's another one of my rules.

Although *The Pilgrim Spirit* was tied to the dock, it was still bobbing up and down in the water. You couldn't tell it was moving from looking at it. But when it was my turn to walk up the gangway to get on board, I could feel the motion. In fact, the boat swayed so much, I had to grab onto the rope so I wouldn't fall over into the water.

"Ahoy there, you scurvy dog," I heard a man yell. I looked around. Was he yelling at me? He couldn't be. I didn't do anything yet!

"That's right! I'm talking to you, you lily-livered flea."

I looked up and standing on the deck of the ship was a large man with a ponytail and a bright red beard. He was wearing a ruffled shirt and a black sea captain's jacket with those gold fringy things on the shoulders. There was no doubt about it. He was definitely talking—make that yelling—at me.

"Aye, I'm talking to you, landlubber," he yelled, putting his face right next to mine. "Did you forget to bring your sea legs, you little worm?"

"No, your honor. I'm sure I packed them."

"You'll call me sir when you speak to me, or speak not at all!" he yelled. He wheeled around and faced the other kids. "And that goes for all you scurvy dogs. You're a sorry lot, and you'll respect your captain or I'll have you flogged!"

None of us could tell if he was being serious or not. Wow. Ms. Adolf had told us that the captain would be acting like real captains did back in the old days. I had no idea it would be this real, though.

"I am Captain Josiah Barker," he said. He pointed to another man, much shorter and chubbier, who was dressed in a leather vest like an old-time sailor. "This is my first mate, Theodore Gladson. We run this vessel and you don't breathe without an order from Officer Gladson or myself. Is that clear?"

We all looked at our feet and muttered something like, "Yes, sir." I noticed that Collin, who was standing right across from me, answered, "Aye, aye, Captain." It figured he'd know the right thing to say.

"Go below and stow your bags," Captain Barker shouted. "And step lively. I want all hands on deck in five minutes. Anyone who's late will pay dearly."

We all hurried down a little flight of stairs and put our duffels away. There wasn't much time to look around, but I could see two big rooms filled with bunk beds. I assumed one was for the boys and the other was for the girls.

"You'll each be assigned a job," said the captain as we gathered up on the deck. It was cold, and a nippy breeze was kicking up from the river. "Mr. Gladson, take over. See if you can shape this ragged crew up."

The first mate stepped forward. He wasn't nearly as scary.

"We'll be traveling round the Cape to pick up a load of hides from California," he said. "It's going to be a rough voyage. Every man and woman aboard needs to work in order for us to complete the voyage."

Luke Whitman put his hand up.

"I don't like to work," he said. "It makes me gag. I thought this was supposed to be fun."

"Mr. Gladson, put that man on first watch," the captain bellowed. "We'll teach him a lesson about working on a tall ship. Fun does not live on my ship."

"You there!" Mr. Gladson said, pointing at Frankie. "You'll join this man in the first watch. He looks like he needs a strong hand next to him. Watch out for pirates and looters who may come aboard and raid us in the middle of the night."

Pirates and looters! This was fun. It was like a movie, but for real.

"Each of you will stand watch," said the first mate. "We work in two-hour shifts. When you're not on watch or asleep, you'll be working on a crew. We'll need galley crew, bilge crew, hide gatherers, deck swabbers, and line handlers."

"Any of you rats and dogs have a problem with that?" the captain interrupted. He flashed us a crazed smile and I noticed that his teeth were yellowish brown, the same color as the sand at Jones Beach.

I saw a hand shoot up in the air. It was Nick McKelty.

"Sir, what about the job of captain's assistant?" he asked.

"Aye," said the captain. "I'll be needing assistants."

"This is the man we've chosen from our class," Nick said, giving me a little shove.

"Let me see your face," the captain growled.

I strutted over to him, trying out my most confident walk.

"Pleased to be of service to you, sir," I said, saluting at the same time.

"Did I speak to you, maggot?" he roared. "No one speaks on this vessel unless I give him permission. Is that clear?"

I didn't know whether I had permission to answer or not, so I just nodded like a bobble-head doll. This was getting a little less fun.

"Any other volunteers?" said the captain.

"I have been chosen from my class, sir." It was Collin Sebastian Rich the Fourth.

Oh, no. Of all the assistants in the world, I had to get partnered with Collin.

I mean, if you were the captain, who would you like better—Mr. Perfect or me?

CHAPTER 12

The first mate saw to it that everybody got to work right away. Frankie and Luke had to stand at the bow of the ship, looking for pirates. They didn't see any of those, but they did see a New York City garbage barge going by. Luke said it smelled like pizza, which makes you wonder what he gets on his pizza. Orange peels and flies? Or maybe potato skins and candy wrappers?

Ashley and her new best friend Chelsea Soccer Camp had to lower buckets into the river to get water to swab the decks. A couple other kids had to polish all the brass on the ship. The first mate took four kids in a rowboat and they paddled over to the next dock to look for hides. Unfortunately, one of those kids was Heather Payne, who finally barfed up her lunch in the East River.

The captain told Collin and me to wait for him on the poop deck while he marched around shouting orders. You're laughing, but it's true. There is an actual place on a boat called the *poop* deck.

"I'm Collin Rich," Mr. Perfect said to me.

"Hank Zipzer," I said, trying to seem taller.

"I know. Ashley pointed you out. She said you're a really cool guy."

Wait a minute here. I was prepared to hate this guy. But he's being nice. Real nice, in fact.

"Can you believe we're standing on the poop deck?" he said.

"They probably call it that because during storms, the captains would get so scared they pooped their pants."

Collin burst out laughing. "Ashley said you're funny too," he said, slapping me a high five. "She's right. So how'd you get to be captain's assistant?"

"A guy named McKelty nominated me," I said. "The class voted. You?"

"My teacher picked me. He said I was tough enough to take it, whatever that means."

Suddenly, I felt a hand on my shoulder. The

captain was back. I gulped.

"This isn't a party, you lazy slugs," he snarled. "Follow me to my quarters, and shake a leg or you'll feel my whip."

I thought he was going a little overboard on the mean captain routine. If he was trying to show us that sea captains in the old days ruled with an iron hand, we got the picture. Maybe he'd lighten up now.

He headed below deck. Collin and I followed. I was looking forward to getting to know the captain away from all the others, when he didn't have to act so mean. I couldn't wait to get my special assignment. I wondered what it would be. What would a captain's assistant get to do that nobody else got to do? Look at old maps and help chart our imaginary course? Look at the stars with a telescope? Or maybe just share a mutton chop at the captain's table.

I have only four words to describe what happened next.

None of the above.

When we got below, the captain made us pull off his boots.

"Polish these until you can see your face in

them," he ordered. "And don't look up until you're done. You there," he growled, turning to me. "Clean the head."

"What head? Your head, sir?" I asked, not knowing whether or not to salute.

He didn't answer, just handed me a bucket and a toothbrush. That was a new one. I'd never heard of washing your head with a toothbrush.

"Excuse me, sir," I said. "But shouldn't you use a toothbrush to brush your teeth, not your head?"

"On a ship, a head is a toilet, you green maggot!" he shouted. I couldn't believe it. He was asking me to *clean the bathroom*! With a toothbrush! I didn't even do that at home.

"I'm going to lie down," he said. "When I wake up, I'll have you dog hairs peel onions for my stew."

He stomped off into his bedchamber and slammed the door.

A lightbulb went on in my head. The captain's assistant wasn't a special job at all. It was a miserable, low-down job. The worst one on the ship, as a matter of fact. Look at what he was having us do: Clean his bathroom, polish his boots, peel his onions. What was next—cut his toenails? No, he wouldn't. That's got to be against the law, even at sea.

Then it hit me. McKelty knew it all along. His brother must have told him exactly what a captain's assistant does. That's why he nominated me—to do the dirty work so he could have a good laugh.

Oh, that Nick the Tick.

I was going to get him for this.

CHAPTER 13

TEN WAYS I'M GOING TO GET EVEN WITH THAT ROTTEN LOUSY PUNK, NICK MCKELTY

1. I'm going to find all the creepy crawly bugs that live on this boat and hide them in McKelty's dinner.

2. After he eats the bugs, I'll tell Old Nick that the creepy crawlies are probably having a great time feasting on his liver.

3. I'll hide Nicky Boy's belt and then get him to do a sailor's jig in front of both classes. His pants will fall down, and everybody will see his G.I. JOE underpants.

4. He'll be so embarrassed, he'll throw himself overboard.

5. I'll find a sea cucumber on the bottom of the river, which I happen to know are

slimy and ooze purple ink. I'll replace his pillow with the sea cucumber, and when he puts his big fat head down on Mr. Cuke, it will pee purple stuff up his nose.

6. No, I can't do that to a sea cucumber.

7. Maybe I'll just have to tell Katie Sperling that Nick rubs diaper rash cream on his chapped kneecaps.

8. I'll tell the captain that the rash on his knees is scurvy and very contagious, so they'll have to lock him up in the ship's jail and throw the key away.

9. When he's asleep, I'll squirt whipped cream in his hand and then tickle his nose with a feather so when he scratches, he smears whipped cream all over his big, ugly face.

10. I'll put his hands in warm water while he's sleeping so he pees up a storm in his sleeping bag.

11. Numbers one through ten are all so good, I could never choose just one. I think I'll have to do them all.

12. I know this is more than ten, but I'm so mad I can't stop myself.

CHAPTER 14

"**What are you writing?**" Collin asked, looking over my shoulder.

"It's nothing," I said, covering up the list with both hands. The last thing I wanted was for Collin to see my horrible handwriting and spelling. He'd think I was a moron.

"You've been hunched over that paper for the last five minutes," he said, lifting one of my fingers and trying to peek under it. "What's the captain going to say when he sees you haven't cleaned the head?"

"He'll say, 'Get cracking, you scurvy dog, or we'll feed you to the sharks below,' " I answered, doing a pretty sweet imitation of the captain's voice, if I do say so myself.

Collin laughed. "You're a genius with impressions," he said. "You sound just like him."

A genius? If he only knew.

"Come on, show me what you were writing," he begged.

"Sometimes I make lists," I said. "This one is how I'm going to get even with that rat punk Nick McKelty. He set me up for this job."

"How?" Collin asked.

"He knew it was a terrible job, so he suggested me. He did it to get me, just to be a punk."

"I can't stand punks," said Collin. "Read me the list."

That was a whole lot better than letting him actually see the list. If Collin looked at my handwriting, he'd think it was a Japanese comic book. And if he ever saw my spelling, I'd have to tell him I'm dyslexic, or he'd think I was a total moron. We were really hitting it off and I didn't want him to think I was "different."

So I read him the list. He started laughing and didn't stop. You would have thought he was watching a "Scooby-Doo" cartoon or something really funny.

"You're too much," he said, holding his sides. "You're a total riot! How do you think this stuff up? I say we blast McKelty. Which number on your list should we start with?"

We? He said we. He wants to help get Nick the Tick. Why? Is he kidding me?

I guess not, because we decided that most everything on the list couldn't possibly be pulled off. But we did come up with something that was perfect. Nothing fancy, just a sweet little plan that would do the job.

For the plan to work, I had to get Nick down to the captain's quarters. That wasn't going to be easy. I knew he wouldn't come if I called him down there. And Collin didn't know him, so it would be strange for him to invite McKelty down. We needed bait to attract him.

But what kind of bait do you use to catch a smelly fatty fish like Nick McKelty?

CHAPTER 15

While we were making our plan, we still had to look like we were working. The captain stuck his head out every few minutes to make sure we were doing our jobs.

"No lollygagging around or I'll have you scrubbing the galley next," he said to me. "And use some elbow grease on those boots, you lazy laddie," he snarled at Collin.

Collin polished the captain's boots and I— are you ready for this—cleaned the bathroom with the toothbrush. I did a really bad job, if I have to say so myself. I don't want to gross you out, so let's just say I gave the old brush a few swishes around the old bowl and got out of there fast.

Ms. Adolf came by to check on us, still wearing her pink pom-pom hat. She said we could take a five-minute break to eat the snack we had brought from home. Dinner wasn't for another hour, and it was only going to be gruel. I had no idea what gruel was. Collin said it was like cream of wheat, only lumpier.

When the captain heard Ms. Adolf's voice, he came barging out of his cabin.

"And who might you be?" he hollered.

"I'm Fanny Adolf, one of the teachers."

"On my ship, you're just another sailor," he said. "Now, Fanny, get your fanny up top and help with the lines. And remove that stupid hat while you're at it."

Ms. Adolf turned all red in the face and those splotches showed up big time on her neck. I smiled. Usually, I would laugh. It was pretty funny to see Ms. Adolf get yelled at. But it was weird seeing this stranger yell at our teacher like that. I was glad when she left.

"And as for you, you scalawag, wipe that grin off your face," he said to me. He stomped back into his cabin and slammed the door.

I got the snack from my duffel and sat there munching on my tofu jerky. It tasted like tree bark, only tougher. But I was so hungry, I just pretended I was a koala bear sitting in a eucalyptus tree chomping down leaves. I was thinking about how koala bears are the cutest animals in the world when I noticed what Collin was having for his snack.

TWINKIES! It was just what we needed to put our plan into action!

I love you, Collin's mom, whoever you are. I love you for packing him Twinkies.

I reached out and grabbed the package away from him before he took the first bite.

"Hey, what's up with that?" he said.

"This is our bait," I said. "McKelty is a Twinkie hog. He gets word we have Twinkies, and he's down here before you can say 'gotcha.' And once he's here, we can do what we talked about."

"Good thinking, Hank," Collin said. "You're the smartest."

Just then, Ashley and Chelsea stuck their heads in the window.

"Collin, you're not going to believe what we've been doing," Ashley giggled.

"Can I hear too, since I am one of your two best friends?" I said to Ashley.

"I was talking to both of you," Ashley

answered. "I meant to say Hank, but only Collin came out."

"Yeah, the two names are really hard to say together."

That came out a little snappier than I had meant it to. I didn't want to be mad at Ashley for liking Collin. I could understand it. He was cool. I wondered what I'd be like if I were perfect like Collin. Would I strut around like some kind of jerk, or would I be really nice like he was?

"We just finished swabbing the decks," Chelsea said. "It's time to change shifts and the first mate said we could be line handlers."

"Poor Frankie. He's bummed out," Ashley whispered to me. "He asked if he could change partners, but the first mate says we have to stay in the same teams all night. So he's stuck with Luke Whitman."

"And that Luke is so gross," Chelsea added. "While they were on watch, he kept picking his nose and trying to wipe it on the ropes. We have to touch those to lift and lower the sails."

"Well, McKelty stuck me with the worst job ever," I whispered back.

I thought I heard the captain moving around

in his room. It sounded like he was coming out again. I had to act fast.

"Ash, we need your help. Go find McKelty and tell him to come here right away."

"Why?"

"I'll tell you later. Just tell him we have Twinkies. Hurry!"

I gave Ashley a strong nudge, something close to a push. She and Chelsea disappeared just as the captain yanked open the door to his room.

"Did I hear someone yammering out here?" he yelled.

"No, sir, Captain, sir," Collin and I both said at once.

"Hand me my boots," he said to Collin. "Bring me my dinner while I get ready for shift change."

He snatched his boots from Collin and disappeared into the bathroom, or head, as we sailors like to say. Two seconds later, McKelty's big face appeared at the window, just like I knew it would.

"I hear you got Twinkies," he said. His beady eyes fell on the pack of Twinkies I had left near the windowsill. His huge hand reached out and swiped them. *Oh, yeah. The stinking fish was taking the bait.*

He stuffed one whole Twinkie in his mouth.

"Haphing a grood time bing za chapn's assisfhunt?" he asked.

"I've really got to thank you, Nick," I said to him. "This is the best job ever."

That got his attention. Nicky Boy stopped chewing long enough to look. A squirt of the cream snuck out of the corner of his mouth.

"Yeah," Collin chimed in, just like we had planned. "While all you guys are up top working in the cold, we're down here hanging with the captain. Telling jokes. Hearing about his adventures at sea."

I could tell this was very confusing to McKelty.

"Really?" he said, swallowing the Twinkie and smearing the cream all over his chin. "He's not mean?"

"Mean?" I laughed. "He couldn't be nicer."

"Yeah, he offered to take us out in the rowboat after everyone goes to bed," Collin said.

"We don't want to be late for that, do we, Collin?"

"You're kidding, right?" said McKelty. There

was some Twinkie goop hanging on the tip of his nose now.

"We're going to get him dinner now," said Collin. "Captain asked if we'd eat with him. It's roast chicken, right, Hank?"

"No, steak," I said. "Thick ones. Oh, and fries."

"Hey, Nick," Collin said. "I hear you guys are going to have to eat gruel."

"That's tough," I said, "because we get chocolate mousse for dessert."

"That's French," Collin said.

McKelty looked like he was going to cry. "But I thought that this job was supposed to—"

He didn't finish his sentence. The big lug was about to give himself away.

"The old captain used to treat his assistants very badly," I said. "But this new captain, he's changed all that. He thinks his assistants should be treated like princes. Isn't that what he said, Collin?"

"No. I think he said kings."

McKelty's little eyes were popping out of his big, thick head. I had him right where I wanted him. It was time to make my move.

"A new assistant was supposed to start at shift change," I said very quietly to Nick, like I was letting him in on the secret formula for Kryptonite. "But he said we could keep the job all night if we wanted to."

"The whole time?"

Collin and I nodded.

"That's not fair," said McKelty. "You're not giving anyone else a chance."

"Hey, why would we sleep in those creaky old bunk beds," Collin said, "when we can stay here on these nice, soft sofas?"

"But keep that between us. We're trusting you," I whispered to him.

"I wanna be the captain's assistant," McKelty whined.

"Hey, who doesn't?" I said. "And thank you, Nick, for thinking of me."

"Please, Hank," begged McKelty. "Let me have the job."

This was the most fun I'd had since Halloween when I dressed up as a chicken and walked into Mrs. Fink's house and asked to be put in her soup.

"If I let you have the job, what will you do

for me, Nick?"

"What do you want, Hank?"

"I want you to stop teasing me."

"Okay."

"And I want you to stop swiping Ashley's Twinkies from her lunch."

He paused a minute.

"Can I have just one?"

"No," I said.

"Okay," he said finally.

"Deal," I said. I held out my hand and we shook. "Congratulations, Nick. You are now the captain's assistant."

I turned to Collin. "I guess we better be going."

Collin and I grabbed our duffels fast. We could hear the captain starting to come out of the bathroom. We had to get out of there.

"See you, McKelty," I said as we bolted out the door. "Give our regards to the captain."

We ran out of the captain's quarters and hid in the bunk room next door. We put our ears next to the wall to see what we could hear. We heard a door slam and then the captain holler.

"Who in blazes are you?" he said.

"I'm your new assistant, sir," answered Nick.

"What happened to those other rascals?" The captain didn't sound happy.

"I know you wanted them for the whole time, sir, but I requested the job at shift change."

"Then what are you standing there for? Make my bed!" the captain roared. "And where is my dinner? When you're done with that, sweep the floor. And unpack my provisions. You look like a lazy dog if ever I saw one."

"But—"

"Keep your mouth closed. No one speaks on this vessel unless I say he can! Is that understood, you over-filled flea?"

I think Nick tried to say something, but all we could hear was the captain yelling. Collin and I tiptoed out of the bunk room and ran up the stairs.

It wasn't until we reached the deck and closed the hatch that we burst out laughing and high-fived each other about ten times.

CHAPTER 16

Frankie saw us laughing like idiots and came over to see what was so funny.

"You look like you're having a good old time," he said without his usual smile.

"We got even with McKelty," I said to him. My sides were hurting from laughing so much. "You should have seen his face, Frankie. He stuck me with the captain's assistant job, and we stuck him right back. It was incredible, wasn't it, Collin?"

"This guy is hysterical," Collin said, slapping me on the back. "I had a blast. And Nick McKelty is a Twinkie-loving fool."

"Zip, can I talk to you for a minute?" Frankie said.

He grabbed me by the arm and practically yanked me over to the railing. "Man, am I glad to see you," he said. "Luke Whitman is driving me nuts. That dude can't keep his finger out of his nose. I've got to get away from him. How about if you and me partner up. I'll talk the first mate into a change and I'll ditch Luke."

I might as well tell you right here and now. I'm not proud of what I did next. But it's what really happened, so I have to be honest with you.

Frankie Townsend is my best friend. He has been ever since we were born. I should have wanted to partner up with him. But I didn't. Nothing against Frankie. It's just that I was having such a great time with Collin. And to be absolutely honest, it felt really good to have the guy everyone wanted to be friends with want to be with me. Collin Rich thought I was smart and funny. He thought I was a genius. Me, Hank Zipzer.

So I said no to my best friend.

"Listen, Frankie, I want to partner up," I said, "but I already promised Collin I'd stay with him."

"Collin?" said Frankie. "You promised Collin?"

"Yeah."

"So let me get this straight. You and Collin

are going to hang together?"

"Yeah, I promised him."

"For the whole night?"

I didn't answer. Frankie gave me a cold stare. I couldn't blame him.

"So that means I'll just be with Luke Whitman and be covered in boogers from head to toe," Frankie said.

I looked over at Collin. He was waiting for me. I turned back to Frankie.

"I want to hang with you, Frankie. Really I do."

"Right," said Frankie. "And my name is Bernice."

He shook his head and walked away.

CHAPTER 17

"**Everything okay?**" Collin asked.

"Yeah, fine," I said. I knew Frankie was mad, and I didn't feel good about that. But what could I do?

We all gathered on deck while the galley crew handed out dinner. Each of us got a portion of gruel, which looked like thin oatmeal and tasted like paper and paste. They served it in wooden bowls and we ate it with a wooden spoon.

I took a bowl and handed one to Collin. I could see Frankie out of the corner of my eye. He was standing with Luke on the starboard side of the ship's deck. Or maybe it was the port side. I couldn't tell because it was too dark for me to see my pinky fingers.

While everyone ate, the first mate talked to us about our next shift.

"Excuse me, Mr. Mate," Katie Sperling said,

interrupting him. "But when do we get our real dinner?"

"This is your dinner," answered Mr. Gladson. "And I would be grateful if I were you."

"You've got to be kidding," said Kim Paulson, letting the gruel drip off her spoon and back into the bowl.

"Tomorrow at daybreak, you'll get your ration of salt beef and ship's bread. Now that's a meal," Mr. Gladson said. "For now, all you get is gruel."

"But I saw some chicken downstairs. And fruit," Ashley said. Good old fearless Ashley. Of course, she'd be the one to speak up.

"Aye, that's for the captain," said Mr. Gladson. "You can't expect him to be eating gruel."

"I don't see why not," said Ashley. "We're eating it."

"How dare you compare yourselves to the captain," said Mr. Gladson, shaking his finger at her. "No more talk! Avast, matey."

"What's that supposed to mean?" Ashley asked.

"It means stop it right now. No lowly sailor talks back to an officer on *The Pilgrim Spirit*."

I could see Ashley getting mad. She was opening her mouth to answer when I saw Frankie reach out and say something to her. I bet you anything that he was telling her to take a deep breath in through her nose and let the anger out through her mouth. It seemed to be working, because Ash didn't say another word. Part of me wished I was over there with them. But the other part felt really proud to be standing there with Collin.

After we finished our gruel, the first mate handed out our next assignments. He told Katie Sperling and Hector Ruiz that they were on galley cleanup crew. He assigned Frankie and Luke to swab the decks. Then he came over to Collin and me.

"You two sailors were captain's assistants on the first shift. Correct?"

"Aye, aye, sir," said Collin. "And I've never had so much fun in my life."

Mr. Gladson seemed surprised. "That's not the usual reaction," he said. "Captain tells me your successor, Mr. McKelty, is having a difficult time of it."

I started to snicker, but stopped when Mr.

Gladson shot me a look.

"Sorry to hear that, sir," I said, trying to look serious. "He wanted that job so badly."

"This shift, you two will be line handlers," Mr. Gladson said. "You'll tie down the ship for the night. You know any knots?"

"No, sir," I answered.

He handed me a book that had been tucked under his arm. It was called *One Hundred Most Useful Nautical Knots*. Oh, boy, I didn't like the sound of that. I had so much trouble just learning to tie my shoes. Tying a boat knot seemed impossible, let alone one hundred knots!

"Study this book," said Mr. Gladson. "It's the first thing sailors read right after they learn to throw a clockwise hitch on a cleat."

What I wanted to say was, *I have no idea what you're talking about.* But instead I said, "Will do, sir. Can't wait, sir."

"Learn the basic knots," he said. "Bowline, square knot, figure eights, cleat hitch. When you've got that down, use a hitch to tie the mooring lines on the starboard side to the two cleats on the dock."

"Will do, sir."

I said it again! What is wrong with you, Hank? Why are you agreeing to do something when you have no idea what you are agreeing to do?

"Which knot should we use, sir?" Collin asked.

"Whatever feels the most secure," Mr. Gladson said.

He started to walk away, and then he stopped to face us again. "By the way, gentlemen. If you complete this assignment, you'll get the line handlers certificate of merit. Captain will give it to you himself. Good luck."

"Let's get busy," Collin said after Mr. Gladson had left. "It'd be fun to show that captain we're not the losers he thinks we are."

Collin and I went up to the front of the boat. Collin picked up some coiled ropes and lugged them over to us. I looked out on the water and for the first time, really noticed where we were. The Brooklyn Bridge stretched across the river right near us. I know it's just a bridge, but, boy, is it a beautiful thing to look at. It's like a shiny, steel spiderweb without the spider, strung with lights. If I turned and looked out into the harbor,

I could see the Statue of Liberty. She was all lit up too. She looked a whole lot better in person than on Principal Love's cheek, I'll tell you that.

"Earth to Hank," Collin said, tapping me on the shoulder. "Mooring lines. Cleats. Knots. Sound familiar?"

I guess my mind had wandered off. It likes to do that.

"Do you have any idea what exactly we're supposed to do?" I asked Collin, snapping to attention.

"Not really. But we can figure it out."

He looked out onto the dock and thought for a minute. He pointed to a big wedge-shaped metal thing sticking up from the dock. A fat rope was tied around it, holding the boat in place while it bobbed in the water.

"I'll bet that metal thing is a cleat," he said. "Do you agree, Hank?"

"Couldn't agree more," I said.

I had no idea what a cleat was. What I did know was that Collin was smart. I could almost see the thoughts racing around his mind.

Collin picked up two loose ropes that were coiled up on the deck near us.

"These must be the mooring lines," he said. "What do you think, Hank?"

"I have to say yes to that," I said. "They look like mooring lines to me. Indeed they do."

I wouldn't know a mooring line from a dotted line. But who was I to disagree with Collin Sebastian Rich the Fourth?

Collin took a flashlight out of his pocket and shined it onto the dock. We could see two smaller metal things jutting up behind the big one.

"I'll bet those are the two cleats he wants us to tie the boat onto," Collin said. "What do you think, Hank?"

"I think that I'm in total agreement."

Hank, you ding-dong! Can't you say anything other than 'I agree'? You're sounding stupid even to yourself.

"Do you know how to tie any knots?" Collin asked me.

"Nope, but we have this book. *One Hundred Most Useful Nautical Knots.* Sounds like a thriller."

"Let's get started," Collin said. "How hard can it be to learn how to tie a knot?"

I flipped open the book. When I looked inside, it was my worst nightmare. No, worse than my worst nightmare. It was my worst nightmare having a nightmare. It was ugly—page after page of diagrams and instructions. There were drawings of right hands and left hands pulling pieces of rope inside and outside of loops. I couldn't tell what was what. The letters and pictures started to move around on the page, just like always. Tadpoles swimming in a pond.

How hard can it be to learn how to tie a knot?

Try impossible.

CHAPTER 18

Frankie, Ashley, and I have a magic act called Magik 3. Frankie is the magician, and we're the assistants. There's this one trick Frankie does where he cuts a rope in two pieces and drops it into a top hat. He waves a magic wand over the hat and says, *"Zengawii,"* which is his magic word he learned in Zimbabwe. When he pulls the rope out of the hat, it's back in one piece!

As I sat there with the book *One Hundred Most Useful Nautical Knots* in front of me, I wished I knew a magic word that would make the stupid rope I was staring at tie itself into a knot.

"Zengawii!" I muttered, giving the coiled rope a kick. Nothing happened.

"What'd you say?" asked Collin.

"I said *Zengawii*, which in Zimbabwe means

why did they make these dumb directions so complicated?"

Collin laughed. "We'll get it, buddy. Just read me the steps."

We were trying to tie a hitch, which is the kind of knot you use to tie a boat to the dock. You'd think that would be easy enough. But noooooo! Turns out there are cleat hitches and clove hitches and rolling hitches and half hitches and other kinds of hitches you never even dreamed of.

We decided to try a cleat hitch. It sounded so right. I looked it up in the table of contents and opened the book to page 97. So far, so good. There were about twenty little complicated diagrams. They were mostly hands with arrows that showed how the hands *would* move if they *could* move. Next to each diagram was a sentence describing what the picture was supposed to be showing you.

I tried to read the first few sentences to myself before I read them out loud to Collin. Every other word was one I couldn't read or pronounce. Like *tension* and *taut* and *counterclockwise*. I knew if I tried to read those directions out loud, I would stumble all over myself and sound totally dumb. I had two choices. I could either confess to Collin that I had a reading problem or I could talk my way out of this.

Guess which one I chose?

"Tell you what," I said to Collin, trying to make it seem like a gigantic light had just gone on in my head. "You read the directions and I'll do the rope-tying."

"Why?" he asked. That was a good question.

"Because," I answered. That was a stupid answer.

I didn't wait for him to tell me that, though. I just handed the book to him really fast. He shrugged and took the book.

From the corner of my eye, I could see Katie Sperling and Kim Paulson looking at us. They were on watch at the stern of the ship, but the person they were watching was Collin. He kept his face in the book, concentrating on the diagrams. I thought it was amazing that he never seemed to notice that girls looked at him all the time.

Mr. Lingg strolled by and smiled at us.

"You boys need any help?" he asked. "I got

a Boy Scout badge for rope-tying when I was a kid."

I wanted to say pull up a chair, Mr. Lingg, and help us figure this mess out. But, instead, I heard my voice say, "We're doing fine. No problem here."

I hate it when my voice speaks without asking me first. Mr. Lingg passed by us and headed over to Katie and Kim.

"Okay, I think I got it," Collin said, looking up from the book. "Step Number One."

I hate instructions that begin with Step Number One, because that means there are seven thousand more steps coming.

"Step Number One," Collin repeated. "Take the line to the ear of the cleat furthest from the load."

Hello! Can somebody translate that into English?

"Step Number Two," Collin read on. "Start your figure eight across the top of the opposite ear."

Check, please. I'm out of here.

"Hey, Collin," I said. "Excuse me a minute. I've got to use the head."

I dropped the rope and took off. I needed Frankie.

I found him and Luke sitting with a group of kids at the stern of the ship. (How about *that* for nautical vocabulary?) They were studying the sky while Mr. Gladson explained how sailors navigate using the stars.

"Psst, Frankie," I whispered, and motioned for him to come over to me. Mr. Gladson stopped talking and frowned at me.

"Are you having trouble with your knots, sailor?" he asked.

"No way. Piece of cake. We'll be getting that certificate for sure. I just need to talk to Frankie for a second."

Frankie didn't look happy about it, but he got up and came over to me.

"I'm in trouble," I whispered to him. "I need help."

"Go ask your new best friend Collin," Frankie said. He started to leave, but I pulled him back.

"Frankie, listen. We're supposed to tie the ship down, but I can't figure the knot out. We're all going to float away."

"No we're not," he said. "Use your head, man. The boat is already tied down. Didn't you see the huge rope wound around that thing-amajig on the dock?"

"It's called a cleat."

"Wow, listen to you, matey. Whatever. You think they're going to let a kid be responsible for making sure we don't drift out to sea?"

He had a point. But Mr. Gladson told us we had to tie down the other two ropes. And there was the line handlers certificate to consider. Collin really wanted that.

"Frankie," I begged. "You know how I am with directions. Come on, you've got to help me. It'll be fun. I'll give you my certificate."

"Oh, now you want to hang out with me?" he said. "Forget it."

"But Frankie—"

"This is the way you wanted it, dude. Tie your heart out."

Frankie went back and took his seat with the group.

On my way back to our station, I ran into Collin. He was heading down the stairs to go below deck.

"Did you give up?" I asked, hoping like crazy that he had.

"I just got cold," he said. "I'll get our jackets and be back."

While I waited for Collin, I leaned over the railing and stared out at the dock. That big rope Frankie had talked about was bouncing up and down as it strained against the cleat. The moon was shining, and I could see the knot clearly. It didn't look so complicated from where I was. In fact, all of a sudden, it was big and clear.

They should make diagrams in books that big, I thought. *Then they'd be much easier to follow.*

Wait a minute. That's it. My brain started going so fast that I thought I *actually heard it clicking.*

Yes! Hank Daniel Zipzer. You just had a brilliant idea.

CHAPTER 19

You have to know this about me. When I get a good idea, I move fast. There's no stopping me. My brilliant idea required that I leave the boat. So I zipped over to the gangway as fast as my short little legs could carry me.

I could see one of the boat's crew members leaning up against the rail guarding the gangway.

Hector Ruiz and a kid from the other school were standing watch on a platform just past the real sailor. I walked past the guard as naturally as I could and over to Hector.

"Hey, Hector, I need you to do something for me."

"I can't now. I'm on watch," he said.

"Hector, this is important. Would you call the guard over and ask him how long your watch period is?"

"I know how long it is. It's two hours."

"Then ask him something you don't know. I need you to keep him talking."

"Why?" Hector asked.

"Trust me, it's for the good of the ship." I was lucky that Hector didn't ask me in what way it was good for the ship. He did, however, say, "Why should I do this for you?"

"Hey, Hector, remember the time . . ." My brain froze. What time? *Think, Hank!*

"What are you talking about?" he asked. "What time?"

"You know, the time," I said, stalling a minute for my brain to catch up with me. "The time I passed that note for you to Tiffany Marshall so you wouldn't get caught throwing it to her."

"So?" Hector said.

"So? Are you kidding? Ms. Adolf looked up just as I handed Tiffany the note. And I took the heat."

"Oh, yeah," he said, smiling. "You went to Principal Love's office for the fifty-third time that week. Hey, did I ever thank you for that?"

"No, but you can now. Just go talk to that sailor, and keep him busy until you see me back on deck."

Hector nodded and called the sailor over to him. The guy turned his back to me and started walking toward Hector's platform. Once I saw them talking, I was off that ship, down the gangway, and on the dock in no time. I scurried right up to the metal cleat with the huge rope fastened to it. I got down on my knees and inspected the knot closely. I looked at it from the top and from the side and from underneath. I could see every loop of it. This was much better than any old diagram. This was studying the real thing, up close and personal.

Frankie and I have put together enough toys for me to know that I learn how to do it best when I actually do it myself. He shows me once, then I do it myself.

I knew that if I could just take that knot apart one time, to see how the rope slipped through the loops, I could do it again. It would just take a minute. The boat wasn't going anywhere in just a minute.

It was a four-step plan.

1. Take the knot apart very slowly.
2. Remember every step.

3. Put the knot back together just the way it was.

4. Go back and impress Collin with how smart I am.

The rope was wet and slimy when I touched it. It practically took up my whole hand just to hold it. This wasn't any little rope. It was as thick around as one of the salamis that hang over the counter in our deli.

I took a deep breath.

Ready, begin. Concentrate, Hank.

I slipped the end of the rope off the cleat and unwound it carefully and slowly. I could see why they call it a figure eight. The rope was wrapped around the cleat so that it looked like the number 8. I kept unwinding it until I could see the bottom of the cleat. There was one funny loop down there. It had a kind of hook in it. I pulled hard on the rope and the hook came undone. It slid off the cleat straight into my hand.

Excellent job, Hank. You were really concentrating. Now just put it back on.

"Hank, where are you, bud?" It was Collin, coming back from below deck.

Hurry, Hank. You don't want him to see you

here. Re-tie the knot. Just like it was.

I threw the heavy rope around the cleat so that it would catch.

Ooops. It's not staying. Why is it sliding off?

"Hank! Get your butt over here," Collin called again. "This isn't hide-and-seek."

I had to move on to the figure eight part of the knot. I wrapped the rope around the cleat in the shape of the number 8.

Wait a minute. That doesn't look like an eight. It looks more like a three. Maybe even a three-and-a-half.

"Hank, the captain's coming up from downstairs for inspection," Collin called.

I had to hurry. I figured that my figure eight was close enough. Now all I had to do was fasten the rope down with a little loop.

Uh-oh. That's a big loop. A really big loop.

I stood back and looked at the knot I had tied. It didn't look exactly like the one that had been there before. I admit it wasn't perfect. But it was good enough. I was sure of that.

At least, I was pretty sure.

CHAPTER 20

I crept up the gangway so quietly that Collin couldn't hear me. Keeping low to the ground, I snuck across the deck until I was in back of him, and then popped out from behind a sail.

"Boo!" I said.

"Where have you been?" he asked.

"I have my places," I said. "An experienced sailor like me knows his way around a ship."

"I brought you this," he said, tossing me my jacket. "In case you're interested, your pocket's glowing."

"It must be my tiny alien brother," I said.

Collin cracked up.

"He begged to come along," I continued. "You know what pests alien brothers can be."

Then I looked at my pocket. There actually *was* a blue light coming from it. Papa Pete's cell phone! I had forgotten to give it back to him. *Typical, Hank.*

Suddenly, we heard footsteps coming toward us.

"Hide your phone! Quick!" Collin said. "The captain's coming."

I turned off the phone and stuffed it in my pocket just as the captain appeared in front of us.

"You two pollywogs tying up the ship for the night?" he said.

"Aye, Captain, but we're having a little trouble with our cleat hitch," Collin said. "Do you think you could help us, sir?"

A funny look crossed his face. It was the same look I get when Ms. Adolf asks me to locate Nebraska on the map and I have no idea where it is.

"You're asking me to help?" he roared.

"Yes, sir."

"Not on your life, matey!" he shouted. "I'm captain of this ship, not a deckhand."

"If you could just—" Collin began, but the captain stomped off really fast. Obviously, he didn't want to be talking to us about tying knots.

We did the best we could with the two

mooring lines. Collin read me the directions, and I tried to remember how to wrap the rope around the cleat. When I was done, the knots looked a little better than the big one I had tied.

"That's good enough," Collin said, looking over my two messy knots. At least he didn't think I was a total moron. "The big line is secure, anyway. It's not like the boat is going anyplace."

I gulped hard. Boy, did I hope he was right.

After that, we had a lot of fun. All the kids got to gather below deck and listen as Mr. Gladson told us an exciting story about a ship that crashed during a storm at Cape Horn. Then it was time to get in our bunks. Ashley went off with all the girls. Frankie chose the bunk next to Ryan Shimozato and farthest away from me.

Collin and I took the bunks closest to the door, because we had to wake up in two hours to stand watch. Our shift was from two in the morning until four. A couple of guys from PS 9 said they had dibs on the bunk next to Collin.

"Back off, guys," he said. "This one's saved for Hank." I felt pretty special.

As we were settling down into our bunks,

Nick McKelty walked by.

"You're a turkey," he said, giving me a poke in the ribs.

"You got what you deserved, McKelty," I answered. "Doesn't feel so good, does it?"

"The captain's a turkey too," he said. "I'm going to tell my dad. He'll get that guy fired."

"Your dad can't do that," Collin said.

"Sure he can," McKelty said. "He's best friends with the mayor of New York."

"Yeah, and my name's Bernice," I said.

Collin laughed really hard.

That was Frankie's line. When he says it, it always makes me laugh too.

I looked over at Frankie. He was hanging out with Ryan Shimozato and a bunch of the guys in our class. They were all watching while he was making a nickel disappear. Frankie was always a lot of fun.

I felt myself wishing that I was over there with him.

CHAPTER 21

Someone was shaking my shoulder. I nearly jumped out of my skin. I had no idea where I was or who was waking me up in the middle of the night.

"Stand up, matey," said a voice. "It's time for your watch."

I rubbed my eyes and looked around. It was pitch-black in the bunk room, except for the candle that Mr. Gladson held next to his face.

"Up on deck with you," he said. "I'll stay below with the others. Hurry, now. Keep a lookout for pirates and looters."

I woke Collin. We put on our jackets and we dragged ourselves out of our bunks and up the stairs. And when I say dragged, I'm not exaggerating. I was so tired, I felt like I was walking through mud.

We pushed open the hatch and went out

on deck. It was cold out there. A pretty strong wind had blown up during the night. The boat was swaying a lot. The sails were flapping in the wind. Funny, they hadn't done that before.

Collin flopped himself down on a bench next to the poop deck. He looked like he was asleep sitting up. I hauled my dead legs over to the railing to have a look around. You never know when you're going to meet a pirate in New York City. You can't be too careful.

I looked out toward the dock. The dock wasn't there.

I ran to the other side of the boat and looked down. The dock wasn't there either.

Oh, no! Where were those docks? They were there when we went to sleep.

We were surrounded on all sides by water. The lights from the pier were far away. The Brooklyn Bridge wasn't right next to us, like it had been. It was off in the distance.

I looked down into the deep black water. I couldn't see much, but I could see the rope dragging along behind us. No knot, no cleat, no land. We had drifted out to sea!

"Collin!" I yelled. "Wake up!"

"What is it, Hank?" he said with a yawn. "Pirates?"

He looked out at the water with a little grin. He rubbed his eyes, and looked out at the water again. The grin disappeared from his face.

"Where's the land?" he asked.

"Way back there," I answered.

"Hank," he said, his voice sounding a little panicky. "We need to do something fast."

I did the only thing I could think to do.

"HELP!" I screamed at the top of my lungs. "SOMEBODY HELP!!!"

CHAPTER 22

I muſt have really ſhrieked my lungs out, because everyone came running up on deck in a flash.

"What is it, Henry?" Ms. Adolf said. She was wrapped in a blanket and still had the pink pom-pom hat on her head.

All I could do was point into the darkness around us. It took a minute for everyone to realize what had happened. Then Heather Payne screamed.

"We're out at sea!" she cried. "I feel seasick."

She ran to the railing and barfed up her gruel.

Not only were we out in the middle of the harbor, we were picking up speed, as well. The wind was blowing hard, filling the sails with cold air. We were cutting through the water at a pretty good pace. And let me just say this: The direction we were heading was definitely not *into* shore.

"Nobody panic," yelled Ms. Adolf in a panicky voice.

"How could this have happened?" shouted Mr. Lingg. You could hardly hear him over the flapping of the sails. I'm not sure why he looked at me, but he did.

"Maybe the knot came loose," I said. "I hear that can happen."

I felt terrible. I knew what had happened. I had untied that big old cleat hitch and then put it together backwards or upside down or maybe even sideways. Whatever I did, the knot wasn't a knot anymore. I was responsible for this mess.

Ms. Adolf and Mr. Lingg had us all put on life vests. After that, no one knew what to do.

"Somebody get the captain," Ms. Adolf said suddenly.

At last, a good idea. We'd just tell the captain to turn the ship around.

Frankie ran down the stairs. Collin went with him. A minute later, they came back without the captain.

"Where is he?" Ms. Adolf demanded.

"He says he's not coming out," said Frankie.

"He's down there with the first mate," added Collin. "He says they're both seasick."

"This is ridiculous," said Ms. Adolf. "I'm going to get him."

"I'll come help," said Ashley. Ms. Adolf didn't object. Mr. Lingg was staying up top to watch over us kids. Ms. Adolf probably felt like she could use a good head down there. And I don't mean of the bathroom type, either.

We were clipping along, heading way out by the Statue of Liberty now. I looked at Lady Liberty's face in the distance, and I swear she was looking right into my eyes. And instead of saying, "Everybody welcome to America," she seemed to be saying, "You did it, Hank Zipzer. You screwed up again."

Ms. Adolf hurried back up the stairs, practically dragging the captain behind her. She had him by the arm. Ashley had Mr. Gladson. Both men were green in the face.

"Captain," said Mr. Lingg. "Take us back to shore immediately."

"I can't," said the captain. He sounded really different. His big shouting voice was gone, and when he did talk, he sounded like he was from Texas.

"And exactly why can't you take us back?" asked Ms. Adolf.

"I'm not a real ship's captain," he answered. "I'm an actor!"

"An actor?" Ms. Adolf said. "What kind of actor?"

"I do musical comedy on Broadway," he said. "I tap dance a little too."

Ms. Adolf turned to the first mate.

"And what about you, Mr. Gladson? I suppose you're one of those silly actor people too?"

"I work in commercials," he said. "Actors do these roles on the ship between gigs. It's steady work."

"I thought I knew his face," Collin whispered to me. "He's that guy on the Smoothy peanut butter commercial."

"Mr. Pea-nut-a-licious," I said. "Wow. He's not very good at that, either."

Ms. Adolf's face had turned as pink as her pom-poms. I think she was mad and scared and confused all at the same time.

"Excuse me, ma'am," the captain said to her.

"I'm going to be sick."

He bolted for the railing.

"You mean to tell me here we are at sea with no help?" Ms. Adolf said to Mr. Pea-nut-a-licious. Her teeth were clenched really tight. "What are we to do?"

It was freezing out there. I stuck my hands in my pockets to try to warm them up. And there it was. Papa Pete's cell phone.

"Ms. Adolf," I said. "I have an idea."

"Be quiet, Henry. This is no time for one of your half-baked schemes."

"But, Ms. Adolf—"

"Did you hear me, Henry?" She pointed to the poop deck. "If you can't keep still, go stand over there and let the grown-ups handle this."

I did go over to the poop deck. But I didn't keep still. I took the cell phone out of my pocket and dialed Papa Pete's number. I figured that since he had been in the navy, he would know how to help us.

My hands were shaking so badly from the cold that I dialed the wrong number by mistake.

"We are not able to connect your call as dialed," said a computer voice.

Before I knew it, someone was taking the cell phone out of my hands. It was Frankie.

"Let me dial that for you, Zip."

I gave him Papa Pete's number. He dialed the phone and handed it to me. It rang and rang. My hand was still shaking.

"Breathe," said Frankie. "Oxygen is power."

I took a deep breath, and by the time I had finished exhaling, Papa Pete picked up.

"Hello," he said with a yawn.

"Papa Pete, it's me. We're in trouble."

"Hankie, where are you?" I could hear he was waking up very quickly.

"On *The Pilgrim Spirit*. It got loose from the dock."

"You're adrift?"

Adrift! I remembered that word from our nautical vocabulary. It meant you've been cut loose from your moorings and you're sailing out of control.

"Yes, Papa Pete. We're very adrift. Make that extremely adrift."

"I'm calling the Coast Guard right now," said Papa Pete. "Where are you?"

"We're just passing the Statue of Liberty. But

we're heading out real fast."

"Are the sails up?" Papa Pete asked.

"Yes. Halfway."

"Hankie, listen to me. I'll call for help. But you have to get the sails down now. If you keep your sails down, you'll stay put until the Coast Guard comes."

"I don't know how to take them down, Papa Pete. And neither does the captain. But he can tap dance."

"The sails are held up by ropes. Do you see which ones they are?"

"Yes, I do."

"Untie the knots and let the rope out. The sails will come down. You can do it, Hankie. Ask the other kids to help."

Papa Pete hung up.

He had a point. I couldn't tie a knot, I had proven that. But I was a whiz at untying a knot. I had proven that too.

I turned to Frankie and Collin.

"Come with me," I said. "We have a job to do."

CHAPTER 23

We sent Ashley to tell Ms. Adolf that I had used the cell phone to call my grandfather and the Coast Guard was on the way. I knew Ms. Adolf wouldn't listen to me, but she'd listen to Ashley. And was I right. When she heard the news, Ms. Adolf didn't even say anything about how cell phones weren't allowed. She hugged Ashley so hard, she knocked her glasses off. Watching Ms. Adolf, I could tell she was really worried about us. In a weird way, that made me feel good.

Collin took me over to his teacher, Mr. Lingg. Frankie came too.

"This is Hank Zipzer," Collin said. "He's the one whose grandfather has called the Coast Guard."

Mr. Lingg reached out and shook my hand. "Good thinking, Hank," he said.

"My grandfather said we have to take the sails down, so we can stay put or at least slow down until the Coast Guard arrives," I told him.

"That sounds like a logical thing to do," said Mr. Lingg. "I wish I knew how to lower the sails."

"If everyone helps me, I think I can do it," I said.

"Take over, Hank," Mr. Lingg said. "You're the captain."

"Can I be your first mate?" Collin asked.

"Only if he's one too," I said, putting my hand on Frankie's shoulder.

Collin put up his hand for a high five. "Two first mates are better than one," he said. Frankie looked at Collin's hand a minute. Then he slapped him five.

"Everyone gather round," Mr. Lingg shouted. "The Coast Guard is on the way. In the meantime, we have to lower our sails. Hank is in charge and will give you instructions."

I climbed the steps going up to the poop deck. Frankie stood on one side of me, and Collin on the other. We looked like those guys in a movie I saw once called *The Three Musketeers*. Except we were wearing tennis shoes and baseball caps, and those dudes were wearing boots, swords, big hats with feathers, and tights. But you get the idea.

"We'll split into two teams," I said. I had to shout really loud to be heard over the wind and the sails. "One team will take the starboard side."

I started to point, but realized I didn't know which side was which. There it was again, that stupid right/left thing. I wonder if any sea captains in the old days had learning challenges?

Thank goodness Frankie saw that I was confused. He stepped in front of me and pointed to the right side of the ship. Starboard, right. Port, left. *Remember that, brain.*

"The other team will take the port side."

Frankie pointed to the left side.

"Your job is to untie all the ropes that are holding the sails up," I said. "This won't be easy, because as you can see, there are hundreds of ropes all over this ship. And the sails are heavy. Three kids to a rope. It doesn't matter which school you go to. Just team up."

"When the sails come down, you'll have to tie them up so they don't flap around in the wind," Collin added.

That was a nice touch. I never would have thought of that. Frankie gave him a high five.

"Hey, a few of you get your flashlights," Frankie added. "We'll need light out here."

"Now, everybody move quickly," I said. The wind was still strong and we were way out in the middle of the harbor. "And, hey, if you see a loose jacket, bring it topside. It's cold."

"Why should we listen to you?" Nick McKelty called out. "You're a turkey."

"You're the one who's a turkey," Ashley shouted back at him.

"Yeah, be quiet, turkey!" her friend Chelsea said.

Chelsea started to gobble. Then Ashley joined in. And, pretty soon, every kid on the whole ship was looking at Nick McKelty and gobbling. Everyone except Heather Payne, that is. She was too busy barfing.

Collin and Frankie and I ran around the deck, making sure all the ropes got untied. I did a whole bunch of them myself, because, remember, I'm really good at that.

As I looked around the deck, it seemed as if the kids—both schools—were standing around sort of frozen, not knowing what to do. Kim Paulson was closest to me and somehow had ended up on Luke Whitman's rope gang. There was a smile on Luke's face that looked like his lips were glued to his ears.

As I ran past them, Kim grabbed my jacket from behind and started yelling, but there was no way I could understand what she was trying to say.

"Try to relax, Kim," I said in my best calm voice. And, believe me, it was not easy to be calm at that moment. "We're going to be fine if we just lower the sails."

"Eeuuw, eeuuw, eeuuuw," she sputtered, and then she started stomping her feet. It looked like her toes were on fire.

"What is it, Kim?"

"The ropes! Eeuuw, eeuuw, eeuuw. Hank, I can't!" she yelled with her eyes tightly shut.

Luke was still grinning.

Ooohhh. Now I got it. Of course. Kim was pulling Luke Whitman's rope, the one he hid his boogers on. Disgusting. Double disgusting.

I took off my scarf and gave it to Kim so she could wrap it around her hands.

"When you hear me count to three, untie the rope and lower the sail," I said. "Can you do that?"

Kim nodded, and I ran.

"Good job, Ryan," I yelled as I passed him and his posse, Justin and Ricky. They had found the rope that was holding the main sail at half-mast. "Wait for me to count to three, and then we'll lower all the sails together!"

I didn't wait for them to answer. We were moving pretty fast down the East River. I couldn't show it, but I was getting nervous.

"Hey, guys, that rope is not going to help us. It's the wrong one. Grab the one next to it."

I ran farther along the deck.

"Hey, you in the blue and yellow parka," I called. "I'm sorry I don't know your name."

"Charlie," he answered back.

"Charlie. Can you help Hector here find the right rope that lowers the front sail?"

"Aye, aye, Captain," he answered while saluting me. Wow, that felt great.

"Thanks," I shouted over my shoulder, heading toward Heather, who was still bent over the railing feeding the fish.

"Are you all right, Heather?" I asked.

She couldn't speak, and looked really, really green. So she nodded and went back to barfing.

"Just hold on," I said. "Help is on the way."

I got back to the poop deck and started shouting.

"Okay, let's get ready!" I shouted. But there was so much noise from everyone talking at once and the wind snapping the sails back and forth that I wasn't sure anyone could hear me. Frankie and Collin were on the poop deck with me and they started getting everyone's attention. They cupped their hands around their mouths and traded off shouting, "Hey!" First Frankie, then Collin, then Frankie, then Collin. Finally, the two classes quieted down enough for me to yell.

"Okay, everyone. Untie your ropes!"

All the kids shot into action at once, and removed each rope from its cleat. Some of the kids weren't strong enough. The wind in the sails was pulling the ropes in the opposite direction and yanked the kids holding them forward across the deck.

"On three!" I yelled. "All together! Are you ready?"

"You bet! Let it rip! Let's go!" came the answers from all over the deck.

"One! Two! Three!" I shouted louder than I had ever yelled before.

When the first sail came down, we all cheered. One by one, the big sails were lowered. As each one came down, *The Pilgrim Spirit* moved slower and slower through the water.

Suddenly, I saw a light in the distance.

"Ahoy there," came a voice from a loudspeaker. "This is the Coast Guard cutter *Orca*. Are you in distress?"

I don't always learn from books very well, but if you tell me something, I'll remember it forever. What I remembered at that moment was the signal for distress that the Coast Guard officer had showed us before we boarded the boat. He said one way you signal distress is by waving your arms up and down over your head.

I ran to the stern of the boat and faced the Coast Guard cutter. I stood right in front of their searchlight beam and waved my arms up and down over my head so hard, I almost took off. Collin and Frankie and Ms. Adolf joined me too. We must have looked like we were doing the wave at a Mets game. But it worked, because the next thing we heard from the Coast Guard ship was this:

"We are sending an inflatable boat out to you. We are coming aboard. Stay calm."

With that, Ms. Adolf grabbed the sides of her pink pom-pom hat and pulled it down over her face. Between you and me, I don't think she wanted us to see her cry, even if it was a cry of happiness.

They sent a skipper to board our ship and steer us into port. He turned us around so we were headed in the right direction. Boy, were we ever glad to see him. You should have seen his face when he saw the pretend Captain Josiah Barker hanging over the ship railing, his face green as the lettuce in Mrs. Crock's teeth.

"When he has finished answering your questions," Ms. Adolf said to the skipper, "ask him to dance. Apparently, he's quite good at tap."

The Coast Guard cutter *Orca* pushed us from behind and we floated into the South Street Seaport harbor. We went very slow. When we reached the dock, it was already morning. A crowd of people was standing on the pier and waving to us. It was all of our parents.

Even from that distance, I could make out one big guy standing in the middle of the crowd. He was wearing red sweats and looked like a giant strawberry.

Papa Pete didn't look like a hero, but I knew that he was.

CHAPTER 24

The good news was that we landed safely. Everyone was totally okay. Oh, as usual, I almost forgot. There was one crisis. Ms. Adolf lost her pink pom-pom hat in the water. There's probably some sharp-toothed eel at the bottom of New York Harbor whose fish friends are all laughing at him because he's wearing that dorky hat.

The bad news was that as we were getting off the boat, Captain Adam McPherson, the commanding officer of the Coast Guard cutter *Orca*, said he wanted to see Collin and me in the harbormaster's office.

Right away.

COAST GUARD

CHAPTER 25

"**You boys care to** tell me what happened?"

Collin and I were sitting in the harbor-master's office facing Captain Adam McPherson, commanding officer of the Coast Guard cutter *Orca*. He didn't yell or anything like the ship's fake captain had. He was quiet and calm, but when he looked at you with his dark eyes, you could tell he meant business.

"Why are you asking us?" I asked.

"Because I'm told you were the sailors on watch when you went adrift," he said. "The Coast Guard needs to know the facts. All the facts."

I don't think I've ever been more nervous in my life. Well, maybe the time when Mr. Gristediano's apartment got totally trashed because I brought Cheerio in and let go of his leash. Mr. Gristediano lost thousands and thousands of dollars of expensive stuff, and it was all my fault. I screwed up big-time that day. Just like I knew I had screwed up big-time last night.

My leg was bouncing up and down like it had a jet engine in it. I wanted to bite my nails, but I had already bitten them all off in the waiting room. Collin didn't seem nervous. That's because he hadn't done anything wrong. It was me. I'm the one who messed everything up, and I was trying to figure out exactly how much of the truth I was going to tell.

Collin went first.

"The captain told us to learn how to tie a couple of knots," he said. "So we did. Then we tied the two mooring lines onto the two small cleats on the dock. I guess we didn't do such a good job."

"You did fine, son," Captain McPherson said. "Those small lines were never meant to tie up the boat. They were just for practice, part of the educational program *The Pilgrim Spirit* provides."

"Really?" Collin said. You could see how relieved he was.

"It's the main mooring that ties the boat down," the captain said. "Did either of you touch that?"

Okay, there it was. The big question.

"No, sir," said Collin. "We wouldn't do that."

I squirmed around in my seat like my pants were on fire. Captain McPherson looked over at me.

"Something wrong, son?" he asked.

"Well, I did kind of touch the main mooring," I said.

"I don't understand," said the captain. "Either you touch something or you don't touch it."

"Well, if that's the way you're defining it, then I guess I did touch it," I said. My forehead was sweating. No other part of me, just my forehead. That's not true, either. My underarms were pretty wet too.

"So that's where you were when I kept calling you," Collin said. He looked upset.

Captain McPherson got up from behind the desk. He went to the window and opened the blinds. I could see the people waiting for us outside.

Three people were standing by a really nice

car. I think it might have been a BMW. They were probably Collin's family. A pretty mom, a handsome dad, and a cute little sister with bright red hair and freckles. Then there was my family, standing by our minivan. My mom with her hair flying all over the place. My dad still wearing his slippers, with his favorite mechanical pencil behind his ear. Emily, who was reading a book on reptiles while she was standing in the parking lot. Papa Pete was there too, looking worried in his bright red sweats.

What would Papa Pete do if he were in my situation? I bet he's never told a lie in his life.

I didn't plan on what happened next. But when I opened my mouth, out it came!

"I didn't mean to do it," I blurted out. Captain McPherson turned from the window and looked me right in the eye.

"What?" he asked. "You can tell me, son."

"I was just trying to figure out how to tie a cleat hitch," I said, almost in tears. "We had this book of instructions, but the truth is, I don't read very well. And I can't follow diagrams, either. See, I have these stupid learning challenges and lots of things that are easy for everyone else are hard for me."

I wasn't almost crying anymore. There were real tears streaming down my cheeks.

"So I untied the main knot, because I thought it would help me learn how to tie a knot. You know, if I took it apart, then I'd see how it worked. But then I couldn't put it back together. I tried, but I guess the knot just didn't hold."

Collin's mouth was hanging open. "Hank, why didn't you tell me all this?" he asked.

"Why didn't I tell you? Are you kidding? I didn't tell you because you'd think I was stupid. I just wanted to be friends, and I didn't think you'd understand because you're so perfect and smart and tall and everything."

I waited for Collin to say something, but he didn't say anything. Not one word. Captain McPherson walked over to Collin.

"Will you excuse us, son? I'd like to talk to this young man alone."

Collin got up and left. I watched him go.

Bye bye, Collin Sebastian Rich the Fourth. I never should have tried to be your friend in the first place.

Captain McPherson sat down on the edge of the desk.

"Accidents happen, Hank," he said. "That's why we call them accidents. You didn't intend to hurt anyone."

Captain McPherson put a hand on my shoulder.

"You made a mistake in not telling an adult what you did," he said. "But then again, you did a lot of things right too. You called for help. You lowered the sails. You signaled that you were in distress. Hank, you showed real leadership. You have a lot to be proud of, young man."

"I'm really glad no one got hurt," I said.

"So am I," said Captain McPherson. He offered me a box of Kleenex, and I blew my nose.

I looked out the window and saw my family. They were trying to look inside, to see if I was okay. Suddenly, I wanted to be with them more than anything.

Captain McPherson walked me to the door of the office.

"You did the right thing in telling the truth," he said. "To me and to your friend."

"You mean my ex-friend," I said.

"Real friends accept you for who you are," he said. He reached out and shook my hand. Boy, did he have a huge hand. As we shook hands, I could no longer see mine. It's like it got lost somewhere in his palm region.

I went outside. Frankie and Ashley were standing right by the door.

"You okay, Zip?" Frankie said.

"We were so worried," Ashley said.

"I'm okay," I said. "Let's go home."

As we walked toward our families, Frankie reached into his duffel and pulled something out.

"I'm supposed to give this to you," he said. "We all got one. It's a souvenir from *The Pilgrim Spirit*."

Frankie handed me the souvenir.

It was my very own copy of *One Hundred Useful Nautical Knots*. Just what I always wanted.

CHAPTER 26

I was so tired, I slept the whole day. When I got up, my mom made me breakfast for dinner. Scrambled eggs and bacon and toast. She knew I was feeling like I had flunked my field trip, so she was being really nice. She didn't even try to throw any tofu in the eggs or pass off her crunchy veggie-strips as real bacon.

After dinner, Frankie and Ashley came up and we sat on the living room floor, practicing our knots. Ashley got bored with the knots and made sailing ships out of rhinestones instead. She glued them on construction paper and made one for her and one for her new friend Chelsea. Frankie taught me how to tie three knots in about ten minutes. It turns out they're not so hard, if you don't have to read the directions.

While he was teaching me the bowline, which in case you're interested is called the king of knots, the phone rang.

"I'll get it," Emily said, diving for the couch to grab the phone. "It's probably Robert."

"If he wants to come over, tell him he has to put Scotch tape over his mouth first," Frankie said.

Emily handed me the phone.

"It's for you," she said. "It's that guy Collin."

"Now if he wants to come over, tell him to hurry," Ashley said.

"Get real, Ash," I said. "He's calling to tell me how much I screwed up his life."

I took the phone and went into my room.

"Hello," I said.

"Hank?" said Collin.

"Yeah."

"Listen, I have a question for you," he said.

Let's see. Which one was it going to be? Why did you ruin my field trip? Why are you so stupid? What's wrong with you, anyway? There were so many to choose from.

"What is it, Collin?" I asked.

"I was wondering," he said. "Do you want to have a sleepover this Saturday?"

CHAPTER 27

We had a great time at our sleepover. Papa Pete took us bowling and got us root-beer floats. We watched scary movies on TV and played Monopoly and told knock-knock jokes until my parents said we had to go to sleep. Oh, by the way, there were three of us. Collin, Frankie, and me. We all got along great together. Ashley slept over at Chelsea's house.

I learned a whole bunch about Collin that night. And I guess about myself too. The most important thing I learned was that Collin likes me the way I am. He doesn't care if I learn differently. He says he doesn't pick his friends by looking at their report cards.

I also learned some other interesting things that night about Collin Sebastian Rich the Fourth.

TEN THINGS YOU WOULDN'T KNOW ABOUT COLLIN JUST FROM LOOKING AT HIM

1. He bites his nails too.
2. He pulls cards from the middle of the Chance pile in Monopoly.
3. He likes the Yankees better than the Mets. That made Frankie happy.
4. At night, he wears headgear the size of a flying saucer. That's how he gets those perfectly straight teeth.
5. His favorite fruit is prunes.
6. He only knows three knock-knock jokes, and two of them aren't funny.
7. He is scared of scary movies.
8. He is also afraid of iguanas.
9. He can't make himself burp unless he's had a Coke first.
10. He is one lousy bowler.

I showed this list to Papa Pete. He says it proves one thing: Nobody's perfect, even the perfect people.

THE END

About the Authors

Henry Winkler is an actor, producer, and director, and he speaks publicly all over the world. In addition, he has a star on Hollywood Boulevard, was presented with the order of the British Empire by the Queen of England, and the jacket he wore as the Fonz hangs in the Smithsonian Museum in Washington, DC. But if you asked him what he was proudest of, he would say, "Writing the Hank Zipzer books with my partner, Lin Oliver." He lives in Los Angeles with his wife, Stacey. They have three children named Jed, Zoe, and Max, and two dogs named Monty and Charlotte. Charlotte catches a ball so well that she could definitely play outfield for the New York Mets.

Lin Oliver is a writer and producer of movies, books, and television series for children and families. She has written more than twenty-five novels for children, and one hundred episodes of television. She is cofounder and executive director of the Society of Children's Book Writers and Illustrators, an international organization of twenty thousand authors and illustrators of children's books. She lives in Los Angeles with her husband, Alan. They have three sons named Theo, Ollie, and Cole. She loves tuna melts, curious kids, any sport that involves a racket, and children's book writers everywhere.